monsoonbooks

CIGARETTE GIRL

Ratih Kumala is an acclaimed Indonesian author based in Jakarta. Her debut novel, *Tabula Rasa*, won the Jakarta Art Council Novel Competition in 2003, and she has published six more novels and short story collections since then. Her novel *Gadis Kretek* (*Cigarette Girl*) has been translated into six languages and adapted into a Netflix series, where she also contributed as part of the writing team. As a screenwriter, Ratih has written for television dramas, films and various digital media. Her latest work, *Saga Dari Samudra*, is a historical action novel.

Books by Ratih Kumala

Tabula Rasa (novel)
Larutan Senja (short stories)
Kronik Betawi (novel)
Gadis Kretek / Cigarette Girl (novel)
Bastian dan Jamur Ajaib (short stories)
Wesel Pos (novella)
Saga dari Samudra (novel)

Cigarette Girl

Ratih Kumala

monsoon

monsoonbooks

First published by Monsoon Books in 2016.
New edition published in 2024.

No.1 The Lodge, Burrough Court, Burrough on the Hill,
Melton Mowbray LE14 2QS, UK.
www.monsoonbooks.co.uk

First published in Indonesian in 2012 by Gramedia Pustaka Utama under the title *Gadis Kretek*, and in English in 2015 by Gramedia Pustaka Utama.

ISBN (paperback): 9781915310408
ISBN (ebook): 9789814625487

Printed and bound in Great Britain by Clays Ltd, Elcograf S.p.A.
26 25 24 3 4 5

For my Grandfather, the late H. Affandi,
and his daughter, Badriyah.

Klobot: hand-rolled clove cigarettes wrapped in cornhusk.

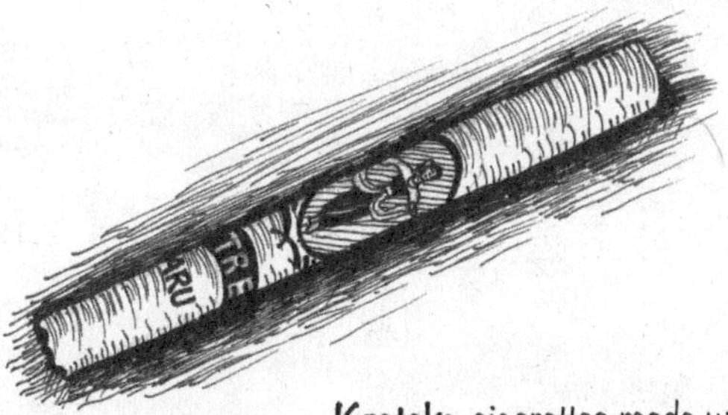

Kretek: cigarettes made with a blend of tobacco and cloves. The Indonesian word 'kretek' is an onomatopoeic term for the crackling sound of burning cloves.

Klembak menyan: cigrattes made with a blend of tobacco, rhubarb root, frankincense and other medicinal herbs.

Contents

Prologue

Jeng Yah

Soeraja was dying. The man had been delirious for days, and he was calling out a name: Jeng Yah.

The name awakened a ghost from the past, a ghost their mother had wrapped up tightly and buried many years ago. When she heard the name, a new side of her emerged, one Lebas had never seen before – she was jealous. Despite the fact that she was no longer a young woman, his mother was most certainly wild with jealousy. It showed in her face, made her seem terrifying. She looked like she could devour anything that upset her, bite into it then swallow it whole.

'I'm the one caring for him during his illness, but it's *her* name he calls!' she griped, her mouth twisting and pouting in fury. She slammed down the bottle of medicine that was to be given to Soeraja that afternoon. Lebas heard his mother grumbling under her breath, whispering between fought-back tears that she wished her husband would die there and then. Lebas never imagined such a curse could come out of his mother's mouth. In the thirty-seven years of his parents' marriage, never once had he suspected that someone had come between them – in fact, if the government were looking for an ideal couple to showcase, he would have volunteered his parents as the perfect choice. And he had believed they had passed down this domestic harmony and tranquillity to their three sons as well.

Lebas and his two older brothers gathered to discuss the situation: 'That woman, Jeng Yah, must have been in the picture long before Mother and Father got married.'

'Why the hell are you uttering that accursed name?' Their mother had overheard their conversation and was staring at them, furious. Her eyes bugged out, and her forehead was creased so her eyebrows were knitted together; her sons' balls began to feel as tiny as sweet-basil seeds. They immediately closed their mouths, ending the discussion, and then scattered, pretending to have more important things to do.

When Soeraja suffered a stroke three years earlier, half his body had died. It was as if the Angel of Death had come to claim him, but had then decided not to complete its duty. At first, right after the stroke had ravaged his body, it had been difficult for them to understand his garbled words: their father had haltingly stammered that he would be better off dead than handicapped. But with therapy, Soeraja had gradually recovered. After a year, he could walk again, even though he still felt no sensation in his arm, and his pronunciation remained slurred. However, he never quite managed to regain control of his emotions – when he laughed, he would keep on laughing, even after everyone else had stopped; when he was moved, as he was when his oldest son, Tegar, finally got married, he sobbed uncontrollably like a ruined man. He had lost his grasp on his emotions. Apparently, the Angel of Death had taken that from him, along with half his soul.

Soeraja lived like that for two years. But then his health suddenly and swiftly declined, and he had been growing increasingly weak since then, as if the remaining half of his spirit was being chipped away at too, piece by piece. As if the Angel of Death was casually stopping by his room, taking a little piece of him each time it visited, and along with it pieces of his memory as well.

And now something frightening had happened. A Pandora's box had been opened: the box containing the name Jeng Yah.

1

Djojobojo Klobot

Idroes Moeria had heard about the ancient prediction from a kyai in his neighbourhood mosque. In the 12th century, a great Javanese king called Djojobojo had predicted that Indonesia would endure three and a half centuries of struggle under the governance of white-skinned men. 'Yes, and he meant the Dutch surely, for they have been making us suffer so!' the kyai had said in Javanese. The king had also foretold that Indonesia would be granted Independence by a yellow-skinned older brother.

Idroes always remembered the prediction, and if his calculations were correct, the Dutch would leave Indonesia the following year. Then, perhaps, Idroes would be able to achieve the future he had always dreamed of. He wanted to raise his economic status and become a small-business owner. He wanted this even though his mother always warned, 'Don't dream too big, son!'

Idroes lived with his mother. He had been forced to become the main breadwinner of his family when his father had died. His mother worked as a servant in their rich neighbour's house, and what she earned was hardly enough for the two of them. At thirteen, Idroes Moeria had started working for Pak Trisno, rolling klobot, cone-shaped cigarettes wrapped in dried-out cornhusks and tied with twine. Gradually, he had risen to take charge of packing them too, and of delivering the orders of klobot to the market stalls and to the shops.

He had grown into a young man now. He had wept when he had seen his father being lowered into his grave, but after that he had never cried again. Even though life with his mother was difficult, and they were barely scraping by, it was as if all of his tears had become buried with his father's body. Idroes Moeria, like most other young men in his community, had dreams of a better future. He was determined to overcome his poverty, so that his mother and wife and their future generations would prosper and be happy. The only problem was that Idroes didn't have a wife yet, and although he fancied Roemaisa, the beautiful daughter of their town's scribe, he wasn't sure that a labourer like him, whose employment involved rolling cigarettes and who couldn't read or write, would ever be accepted by a woman like her.

Ever since he had started working for Pak Trisno, Idroes Moeria had been quietly observing him. He deeply respected his middle-aged employer and thought of him as a sort of father figure. Idroes discerned that his employer's lifestyle was fairly affluent from selling klobot in M Town, where they lived. He also noticed that most of the popular brands of cigarettes were produced in other cities, especially in Kudus. People called his cigarettes simply 'Trisno's Klobot' because the owner hadn't given his cigarettes a special brand name. Idroes Moeria wanted to own a klobot business of his own someday, but he intended for it to be more successful than his employer's; he had what people call a vision and a mission. Idroes Moeria had even picked out a name for his business and had ideas for unique packaging that would make people take notice of his product.

When it came to Roemaisa, what had begun as an interest in the girl had soon blossomed into love. She seemed different from the other girls in M Town, who were always giggling together in groups. Roemaisa was quiet and pretty and she usually went out alone, her body language like that of a mellow cat. Without a doubt, there were many other young men who had their sights set on her too and wished for her to be their sweetheart. When she passed Idroes Moeria on the street she would glance at him, smile warmly and then bow her head and keep walking. But he had taken note of that smile, and he knew that Roemaisa didn't smile like that for other men. She smiled only for Idroes Moeria. Even though they had never really talked to each other until now, he was sure that Roemaisa was speaking to him with her gaze and her smile. He was certain that she was already falling in love with him too.

As the daughter of a scribe, Roemaisa's life was fairly prosperous, much more so than that of a labourer's. So if Idroes Moeria wanted to marry her, he would have to assure her a good and contented life with him. Roemaisa's parents would never give her to a man who couldn't take proper care of their daughter. What's more, she could read and write the letters of the alphabet. Idroes had discovered this to his disappointment when, one day, he had caught sight of Roemaisa helping her friend read a love letter. This made him feel inferior and lose confidence in himself, for he himself could only read Arabic letters – and even then, like most others in M Town, he didn't understand what they meant. Every child was taught to read the Qur'an in their neighbourhood mosque, so everyone could sound out Arabic, but they did not learn anything else unless they went to a public school.

A friend of Idroes Moeria, also a klobot roller, was eyeing Roemaisa as well. His name was Soedjagad. And even though the two of them had been playmates since childhood, when it came to winning over Roemaisa, Idroes Moeria considered Soedjagad his rival, perhaps even an enemy. Idroes would sneer to himself that Soedjagad was a stupid man who was kabotan jeneng, or had a name that was too big for his personality. His name meant 'the origin of the universe'. Idroes Moeria guessed his parents must have held dozens of selamatan rituals for him in the hopes that their son would live up to such a name.

* * *

When Idroes Moeria heard that the Dutch were leaving and that the big-brother nation of Japan had finally arrived in Indonesia, he rushed to the mosque and prostrated himself in gratitude. Finally, he was one step closer to achieving the dream he had envisioned for so long. The Dutch had even surrendered Surabaya to Japan – the big brother was so strong it had been able to chase the Dutch out of Indonesia in no time at all. Even though Idroes Moeria had never seen the Japanese with his own eyes, he felt incredibly grateful towards them.

It was fitting to celebrate this momentous occasion with a cycle ride past the scribe's house, so Idroes could try and catch a glimpse of Roemaisa sitting by the window. That day, the weather in M Town was pleasant and sunny. He slowed his bicycle when he rode past the house, and his heart rejoiced when he saw that the front door was open and that Roemaisa was sitting in the front room reserved for guests. He felt he was floating up and off his bicycle, carried away with happiness. But then his heart sank suddenly when he caught sight of who was sitting in the chair across Roemaisa: Soedjagad.

Idroes Moeria came to a halt at the end of the street. Confusion and jealousy wrenched his heart. What was that worthless guy doing at the scribe's house? More importantly, why would Roemaisa be allowed to sit with him? Idroes was aware that up until now his enemy Soedjagad had never visited Roemaisa's house, even though he desperately wanted to win the affection of the girl.

Perhaps he was mistaken? Perhaps the man sitting in the front room wasn't Soedjagad after all? Idroes Moeria gathered his wits and courage, and he decided to turn his bicycle around and check again if what he had seen was indeed true. As he passed by the house for the second time, he slowed his bicycle to be certain his eyes weren't playing tricks on him. This time he saw even more clearly, that it was in fact Soedjagad sitting there, and that the scribe and his wife sitting were seated next to him, and of course there was Roemaisa too. Was Soedjagad …? Idroes Moeria couldn't dare finish his thought, afraid that his suspicions were correct and his worst fear was coming true – that Soedjagad was, at that very moment, asking for Roemaisa's hand.

That night, Idroes Moeria couldn't sleep. It started to rain despite the earlier good weather, as if the universe knew what was happening in his heart. What good was it that the Dutch had left and the Japanese had arrived if Roemaisa was already betrothed to another? Idroes vowed to stay a bachelor until the day he died if Roemaisa was married off to Djagad. Perhaps he had a vision and a mission, but he had been too slow in carrying it all out. Someone who had bigger balls than him, someone named Soedjagad, had proposed to Roemaisa first. But what if he was still mistaken? Perhaps he had just been paying her a visit. But if it was only an ordinary visit, what was the purpose of it? Idroes Moeria lay fretting in bed, tossing and turning restlessly. He couldn't sleep no matter how hard he tried. There was only one thing left to be done: he would have to speak with Djagad about the visit.

The next day, Idroes Moeria asked Soedjagad whether he had gone over to the scribe's house the previous day. The man was taken aback and asked how he knew about it. Idroes replied that he had just happened to be passing by. But Soedjagad was not forthcoming when he enquired about what had taken him to the scribe's house. He said that he had to deliver some klobot the scribe had ordered. Could that be the truth? Since when was the scribe buying large orders of klobot? Djagad didn't reply. He simply kept rolling his cigarettes in silence. Idroes Moeria concluded that none of his rival's answers had made any sense.

After he was finished with his rolling, Idroes Moeria sought out Pak Trisno and asked him whether it was true that the scribe wanted to become a distributor for Trisno Cigarettes. The employer shook his head in confusion and wondered where Idroes had heard such a thing. Idroes then asked Pak Trisno if the scribe had bought a large order of their cigarettes. The employer replied that he had not received an order from the scribe at all. Now Idroes was convinced that Soedjagad had been lying, and he could not stay calm any longer. As the workday drew to a close and it was time for them to head home together, it was clear to Idroes that Djagad was avoiding him.

But God had his own plans. When Idroes Moeria was sitting on the grass outside Pak Trisno's house, alone, smoking his klobot and mulling over what had happened, the very girl he was thinking about walked past him. He quickly tossed his cigarette to the ground and hurriedly stamped out what was left of it. He stood up quickly and flashed Roemaisa a respectful smile. The girl walked by quietly as usual, first bowing her head and then glancing up at him to give him a sweet smile then looking down again and continuing on her way. Idroes Moeria was, as always, struck by her beauty. He wanted to say something to her but, as always, his throat closed up and he felt like he was choking.

He had once again missed the opportunity to greet her, let alone ask about the previous day's incident. She was already gone, walking away from him. Idroes Moeria was not following Roemaisa, but he *was* admiring her back and watching her go when suddenly a miracle came to pass: Roemaisa stopped and slowly turned around to look at him. Idroes was dumbstruck. His throat was still caught, even though he desperately wanted to speak to her. Then Roemaisa spoke to him. She said, in the most melodious voice that he had ever heard in his short life, 'Learn to read.' Then she turned again and walked on, and this time she was truly gone.

For a moment Idroes Moeria simply stood there, stunned by what he had witnessed. God was truly kind to him, he thought. The cloudy day was turning bright once again. He hopped onto his bicycle and pedalled home briskly. That night, he thought about what Roemaisa had said to him ... Learn to read. Learn to read. Learn to read. He realized that she wanted him to learn to read the letters of the alphabet.

The problem was, however, Idroes Moeria didn't know who could teach him. He asked his friends whether any of them knew how to read, but they all shook their heads. When he asked Soedjagad, the man turned away with a sour expression on his face. Finally, Idroes Moeria decided to visit the local public school – he was determined to learn to read, even if it meant that he would have to take time off work and risk losing some money. But when he arrived at the school, he was completely shocked to find that the building was deserted and in complete disarray. An old man was walking past and informed him that the Japanese had forced the public-school teachers to work for them, and so the school had been shut down. Also, there were rumours that more people were being forced to work for the Japanese.

Forced. Forced? It was hard for Idroes Moeria to accept that word in association with the Japanese. Hadn't they freed Indonesia from the Dutch? If the Japanese had asked politely, people would have obliged; they didn't need to be forced.

But Idroes Moeria's questions were answered when he returned to work the next day. Pak Trisno declared himself out of business and no longer a cigarette merchant. He announced that all the cigarettes that had been made the previous day had been seized by the Japanese, to be used as war capital. War? War with whom? Idroes was confused once again. The entire tobacco industry was apparently plummeting because the Japanese were confiscating all the raw tobacco directly from the plantations. The employer apologized to his workers, for he wouldn't be able to pay them for their last week of work. He had no money left; the Japanese had taken all of his belongings as well. The workers dispersed with anxious and worried hearts.

That afternoon, Idroes Moeria and some of his co-workers, including Soedjagad, went to meet with Pak Trisno and express their sadness at his current condition. He received them with a haggard face but said that he was lucky he wasn't being ordered to fight for Japan. The word on the streets was that the Japanese were capturing people and taking them to Soerabaia, to a place called Koblen, and putting them in forced labour camps. Pak Trisno reiterated that he had no money left at all, that he had nothing in his possession but two big baskets filled with dry tobacco. He hoped to sell them, even if for a cheap price. He asked that his workers spread the word about the tobacco so someone would come forward to buy them.

As Idroes Moeria went home, his head was crowded with thoughts. He had been saving up some money, little by little, from his cigarette-rolling wages. That night, he returned to Pak Trisno's house and expressed his desire to buy the leftover tobacco. He took out his savings and held it towards his former employer, 'This is all I can afford.' Pak Trisno cried when he saw the money. It was far less than what he would have been paid by another buyer, but he accepted it.

'All I have is the tobacco. There are no cornhusks for rolling,' he said.

'That's alright. I can prepare the husks myself.' Pak Trisno nodded, touched by Idroes Moeria's answer. Then the youth continued, 'But Pak … There is something else I need from you.'

'What is it?'

'Please teach me how to read the alphabet,' Idroes requested.

Pak Trisno agreed, he would teach Idroes Moeria how to read. That night, Idroes went back and forth between Pak Trisno's place and his own, hauling tobacco. He borrowed an ox cart to carry it. He was extremely excited to begin his own klobot business. Pak Trisno had even thrown in some leftover cloves for free.

At the crack of dawn, Idroes Moeria visited the labourers as they were starting work in the cornfields. He bought some cornhusks from them for a cheap price. Then, placing the cornhusks in a woven winnowing tray, he set them to dry on the roof of his house. After that, he went to Pak Trisno's house to learn to read the alphabet. His old employer had written the letters on a chalkboard. Idroes had just finished memorizing the string of vowels, A-E-I-O-U, when a guest arrived: it was Soedjagad.

As he greeted Pak Trisno and engaged him in some small talk, he stared at Idroes Moeria, who was trying to copy Trisno's handwriting, Idroes did not look up, but eavesdropped on the conversation.

'Pak, I found a buyer for your tobacco, if you are still interested.'

'Oh, you're too late, my boy!'

'What do you mean too late, Pak?'

'Somebody else has already bought it,' he said in Javanese.

'Who?'

'He did.' Pak Trisno pointed to Idroes Moeria, and the latter in turn, whether he wanted to or not, had to look over at the men and nod in acknowledgement.

'For whom did you buy the tobacco?' Soedjagad asked.

'No one. I bought it for myself.'

'Why would you want to buy so much? You want to smoke it all until you pass out?'

Idroes Moeria only smiled in response. He had no intentions of divulging his plans to anyone. Especially not to Soedjagad. He wanted everyone to just wait and see what he could do. Meanwhile his rival left disappointed, with no commission.

At midday Idroes rode back home, mentally reviewing the few letters of the alphabet he could remember from the day's class. He didn't forget to go past Roemaisa's house, but noticed that the front door was closed. He wanted to call out to the girl, to shout out proudly that he was learning to read, but instead he peddled his bicycle back to his own house and proceeded to collect the cornhusks off the roof. He borrowed an iron from his mother and set out to flatten the dry husks with extreme care.

After that, he cut the husks into sheets, one by one. When he was finished with the task, Idroes Moeria was satisfied to see the pile of klobot he had made: spread out before him, they covered the surface of his bed. He was positive that his dreams of becoming a cigarette merchant would lead him to a bright future. He slept with a light heart that night, imagining all the money he would earn. With that money, he would ask for Roemaisa's hand.

The next day, after returning home from his reading lessons at Pak Trisno's house, he rolled more cigarettes. By the end of the day, he had made four hundred. That's not much, he thought, but then he had only worked for half the day. When he had been employed with Pak Trisno, he had been able to make about one thousand two hundred klobot during the course of a single day. A few other workers, who were more diligent and had more agile hands than Idroes, could roll up to two thousand. They didn't even need to look down as they rolled – not until they were finished and had to tie up the cigarette with some hemp twine. Actually, Idroes Moeria did have the energy to roll more cigarettes, but he was forced to stop working before the sun set in the west and then had to lay out the ones he had rolled for drying. Then, he had to splash some saccharin on them so they would taste sweet. This also made them water resistant.

When the sun began to be truly miserly with its rays, Idroes Moeria resumed his klobot-making inside the house. He didn't want any dew or rain to spoil his efforts, especially since most of the cigarettes weren't completely dry yet. The next morning, when the dew had completely evaporated, Idroes would take the cigarettes back out and place them in the sun before going to study at Pak Trisno's.

From the pile, he picked out a klobot that seemed dry and

almost ready. He lit a flame and held it to the tip of the cigarette, then inhaled the taste of something wonderful: his very own klobot. His gaze never wavered from it … Soedjagad's comment echoed in his mind: 'You want to smoke it all until you pass out?' Idroes Moeria chuckled to himself. He already had thought of the best name for his cigarettes: Klobot Djojobojo, named after the ancient prophet king. Yes, that was what he would call them.

Secretly, Idroes was quite proud of himself. He was his own boss now. He no longer worked for anyone. He could diligently do everything himself to make his business a success. Because he didn't have enough money to make a label or a hard pack, Idroes decided to buy a few sheets of brown paper, cut them and then use the pieces to wrap a bundle of ten cigarettes. He took a pinch of sago flour and heated it over a flame until it liquefied, then used this as glue to bind the brown paper packaging he had made. Idroes Moeria intended to supply his klobot to shops and to stalls in their town's market, but it turned out this wasn't as easy as he had expected. At first, the ladies working at the shops didn't trust his product because his packaging looked amateur – it didn't even have a label, and it was common knowledge that any product, including clove cigarettes, was first introduced to potential customers by its packaging. Finally, the Chinese man who owned the shops became involved. He proposed that he would be willing to sell the klobot if he could try one of them for himself first. Idroes Moeria agreed. The shop owner lit a match and began to smoke his klobot.

'Have you even used cloves? I can't sell your cigarettes. People with asthma aren't going to want them. They won't feel better after smoking them!' the shop owner protested, speaking in Javanese with his unique Chinese accent. The man said that most of his customers who came to buy klobot with cloves in them believed these cigarettes were a remedy for their asthma. The cloves inside them were known to be soothing, with antiseptic and anti-inflammatory properties.

Idroes Moeria knew he had only mixed in a small amount of cloves with the dried tobacco, but that was because Pak Trisno had only given him a small amount of left-over cloves, and he had no money to buy any more.

The Chinese man agreed to sell his klobot in his shops if Idroes promised to use more cloves in his next batch. Idroes Moeria agreed to do this. He was not complacent, and he saw all feedback as being useful for his business. It was important to know what his customers really wanted.

Soon, he was able to read and write, and he wrote out the name 'Klobot Djojobojo' on the brown paper he used to wrap his cigarettes. Idroes Moeria began to record all of his expenses in a notebook: he organized it neatly, drawing a line down the edge of the page with a ruler to keep his sums straight. His handwriting was gradually improving too. At first he had only been able to write in pencil, because he had to erase his mistakes often, but now he was using a pen. Every three days he went back to the shops and the stalls in the market to enquire about how much of his supply had been sold and to collect his money from the sales.

Idroes Moeria paid close attention to the needs of his customers. Just as he had promised, he used more cloves in the klobot he supplied to the shop owner, but he didn't use as many for the ones he sold in the market. Idroes Moeria separated the two, even though he used the same brown paper to package both cigarettes. What's more, he noticed that the farmers preferred to buy tingwe, also known as linting dewe, loose tobacco they could roll into cigarettes themselves. Many of them smoked klembak menyan, tobacco mixed with rhubarb root, frankincense and other medicinal herbs. Idroes decided to do a market test: he rolled a few klobot, wrote 'Klembak Menjan Djojobojo' on the pack, and he decided to use red wrapping paper for these cigarettes, while using white for his regular clove klobot. All of these packs, of course, he still labelled by hand. This was his first attempt at diversifying his products.

One day, when he was bringing his products to the market, there arrived a courier supplying another new brand of klobot to the merchants who had become Idroes Moeria's regular customers. The courier was trying to convince them that his new klobot was delicious and even announced a discount of fifty percent to anyone who bought his wares that day, which meant the merchants could make a big profit. When they examined the packs of the new klobot, they saw that they were wrapped in thick and crisp brown paper, which made them look sharp, even though there was no label attached to dress up the pack. This new klobot had hand-lettered packs, just like Klobot Djojobojo, but its letters stood neat, regular and straight, unlike Idroes Moeria's packs, where the writing was a messy scrawl, even though he had tried his best. Idroes Moeria read the product's brand name: Djagad's Klobot. Djagad? Could it be?

'Who made these?'

'Mas Djagad ... That's why he named them Djagad's Klobot. Would you like to buy some, sir?' the courier offered.

'Djagad? As in, Soedjagad?' Idroes Moeria asked, just to make sure.

'Yes.' The courier glanced down at the pack of Djojobojo Klobot that Idroes Moeria was holding.

'Is your name Djojobojo?' Apparently the man could read.

Idroes Moeria shook his head and answered curtly, 'No.'

'But you have named your cigarettes Djojobojo Klobot?'

'Yeah, Droes,' one of his regular distributors chimed in, 'I was also quite surprised that you used that name for your brand ... because it's someone else's name. Your name is Idroes Moeria, isn't it? If you used the name "Footstool" or "Bamboo Thicket" or "Star", it would be no problem.'

'I like the name Djojobojo, sister,' Idroes Moeria smiled at the merchant, and then he asked the messenger, 'So now Djagad can read and write, is it?'

'Oh, no, Mas,' he said. 'He has hired someone to do the writing for him, so that it would look good.' That means he can't read yet, thought Idroes Moeria to himself.

'And did you write yours yourself?' someone else asked, pointing to his pack. Idroes Moeria gave a small nod. He hoped the people weren't secretly mocking his handwriting. More importantly, he hoped the courier would not report back to Djagad that the handwriting on his packs was much neater than Idroes Moeria's.

Suddenly, he found himself filled with anxiety. He vowed that someday he would have enough money to afford flashy packaging for his cigarettes, or at least labels to stick on the packs.

'So would you like to buy some, sir?' The courier still dared to try and sell his goods to Idroes Moeria. At first, he was angered by the man's audacity, but then he thought about it for a moment and decided to buy some of Djagad's klobot – after all, they were being offered for half their price. And as he did so, he realized that in addition to all the klobot sellers that had been selling in their market for a long time, he now had a new competitor: his old friend Soedjagad.

2

Lebas

Lebas was visiting home after three months. He lived in Jakarta, as did his family, but he preferred to stay in his own apartment and pursue his creative endeavours without distraction or interruption. His older brother, Karim, had called him several times to inform him about their father's condition, but Lebas hadn't visited right away. He hadn't realized their father was in such bad shape. After all, Lebas had heard that he was being cared for at home and that his brothers were running the family business as usual, and were even leaving town on business trips. He had finally decided to visit the family home on the day he knew Tegar was returning from a trip to Singapore. There was something Lebas needed to discuss with his brother: work affairs that had nothing to do with their family's cigarette factory.

Soeraja was lying in bed. The curtains in his room were closed, as if even a ray of sunlight could hurt him. Because of this, the stale and putrid smell of pain clung to the air around him, even though a servant came in every day to clean the room. Worried, Lebas put aside his intention to talk business with Tegar.

Instead, he said to his brothers, 'I don't know how much longer our father has. What will happen if he suddenly leaves?'

'What do you mean "leaves"?' asked Tegar.

'You know, leaves ... dies.'

'Astagfirullah, Allah forgive us! Lebas, you shouldn't say such horrible things!' Karim warned.

'How is that horrible? It's true, isn't it? Everyone who lives must die, someday.'

At first, his two older brothers didn't respond. Then, Karim broke the silence. 'So, what do we do now?'

'I think we have to ask our mother about Jeng Yah,' Lebas said.

'Didn't you see her face when Father called out that name? She will slaughter you if you ask her.'

Lebas's hand moved unconsciously to his neck on hearing the word 'slaughter'. Perhaps his mother might just be willing to use a machete to decapitate anyone who uttered the name Jeng Yah – so consumed was she by her jealous rage.

'But if our father dies, and he's not at peace, what then?' Lebas pressed.

'Well, that's it then. It's called dying. He'll die.'

'Yeah, but it can't happen that way, Mas,' Lebas insisted stubbornly, albeit still addressing his older brother with respect. 'If he dies with unfinished business weighing on him, then his soul will be left wandering in the afterlife.'

Tegar smacked the side of his brother's head with his palm. 'You've worked on too many horror films!' he said to Lebas, annoyed.

'Mas, just look at our poor father,' Lebas cried out, fixing his hair. 'He keeps calling for Jeng Yah. Who knows ... perhaps he wants to see her, or perhaps he just wants to know how she's doing. But whatever it is, this is his dying wish. How could we disregard our father's final request? Could you really bear to do that, Tegar?'

'But his final request is driving our mother insane!'

'Well, if circumstances were different, and if it was our mother's dying wish to meet an old sweetheart, then you'd better believe I would try to fulfil her last request too,' Lebas said, trying to persuade them.

'It does seem like Jeng Yah is our father's old girlfriend, doesn't it?' wondered Karim.

The word 'sweetheart' had just slipped out of Lebas's mouth, a conclusion he had jumped to when he heard Soeraja call out the name. But he was growing increasingly sure of this now. 'Of course it's an old girlfriend! Nothing else would have made our mother so jealous.'

'If that's how it is ... then you will have to ask Mother about Jeng Yah!' Karim said, pointing at Lebas.

'Huh? Me? Mas Tegar should do it! There's no way our mother will slaughter him. After all, he's the one who runs the factory. But if I do it, she will definitely attack me ... I'm not that useful, am I? I am expendable since I have no influence in the company.'

Tegar heaved an annoyed sigh. He knew Lebas was right. Tegar was indeed the golden child of the family, the child on whom their parents pinned all their hopes. He was the firstborn they had urged to become the successor of the family business: Djagad Raja, or Great Universe cigarettes.

'Why don't we just ask Father about Jeng Yah?' suggested Karim.

'That's a great idea!' said Tegar.

'No way!' Lebas burst in. They all looked at each other blankly, and before Tegar could say anything else, Lebas continued, 'Mas, how could we possibly talk to him about it? He's slipping in and out of consciousness.'

'Well, we should at least try.'

Lebas considered this for a moment. Then, he gave in. 'Yeah, okay. Perhaps, it might be better to get some information from him first, before we approach our mother.'

The brothers were in agreement finally. As Tegar got up to leave, he said to Lebas, 'You're watching over our father tonight, aren't you? Try to find an opportunity to ask him.'

'Yup, you got it!' Lebas answered confidently. However, he looked nervous.

'And be careful. Don't let Mother find out,' Tegar warned.

Lebas nodded. 'But if I fail, then you'll give it a try, right? Basically, whoever gets the opportunity to ask Father will do it? That's our Plan A.' The brothers agreed.

'So what's Plan B?'

'Plan B is that Mas Tegar will ask our mother about it,' Lebas said.

Tegar frowned and turned away. He was annoyed again. When he left, Lebas turned to Karim, 'Great, I've pissed him off. It will be even more difficult now to approach him about my work.' When Karim flashed him a questioning look, Lebas proceeded to show him a PowerPoint proposal on his MacBook.

Karim sighed. 'You know very well this matter can't come directly to me. You will need to talk to Mas Tegar.'

'Can't you help me out a little bit?'

'Not really. This is Mas Tegar's decision to make.'

* * *

Lebas cleaned himself up and wore the smartest clothes he owned.

He was to meet Tegar at his office. When he arrived, there were a few other people in the waiting room, all familiar faces. The first was Ipung Wardoyo, a commercial director, who didn't recognize Lebas of course. The second, Maria Johansyah, was a feature-film director currently venturing into theatre production. Djagad Raja clove cigarettes often sponsored large arts events like concerts and theatrical performances, and Karim was usually the one who took care of all of this, but the decisions were not his alone – Tegar had more say in such matters. Perhaps the visitors had come over to pitch some concepts to Tegar.

'Oh, Mas Lebas! You're here too?' It was Jul, an assistant director who had previously worked on one of Lebas's sinetron television dramas.

Lebas smiled. 'Yes, Jul. What brings you here?'

'Pitch meeting. You are here for that too, right?' Lebas had no idea there was a pitch meeting happening that day. He smiled again to mask his surprise. Jul continued, 'I'm working with Ms. Maria, Mas. I'm learning to make commercials. It's crazy that Djagad Raja cigarettes is having its anniversary, isn't it? There must be some real money set aside for advertisements! It's not like working on the sinetron, is it? There, we work every day but earn little. If we want to make a lot, then we shouldn't work in soaps.' Jul laughed. Then he glanced over at Ipung Wardoyo and dropped his voice to a whisper, 'But it's stiff competition. Big time commercial directors are pitching too.'

So it was the day of the formal open-pitch meeting for the Djagad Raja cigarette commercial, and all the filmmakers in town knew about it. Except for Lebas. A young woman appeared from the inner office. It was Sabrina, Mas Tegar's secretary. She smiled warmly at Lebas.

'Hello, Mas Lebas. I haven't seen you in a long time. Are you here to meet with Mas Tegar?'

'Yes, is he in?'

'He is.'

Jul nudged him, whispering, 'You know Mr Tegar?'

'He's my older brother.' Lebas flashed him a grin then strode into Tegar's office, leaving Jul staring after him in surprise. Considering that Lebas had never been involved in the family business, it was hardly surprising that most people didn't recognize him as heir to one of the biggest cigarette companies in Indonesia.

On the walls of Tegar's office hung posters from the different arts events that Djagad Raja had sponsored over the years. Tegar was quite proud of them.

Lebas dreamed of making a top-of-the-line film some day, a high-budget movie with real artistic and moral value featuring top stars like Dian Sastrowardoyo, Nicholas Saputra, Kinaryosih and Lola Amaria – or, if he had to use senior actors, Didi Petet, Christine Hakim and Tio Pakusadewo. Unfortunately, even though Lebas belonged to a wealthy family, it was not easy for him to realize his dreams. From the outset, he had stubbornly tried to prove that he could stand on his own two feet and become a director without needing any of the Djagad-Raja family money. So when he returned home from college in America and was approached by a production house that liked his student short-films and wanted to give him the opportunity to work as a film director, he accepted the offer immediately.

The producer promised Lebas that he would be allowed to make the kinds of films he wanted as long as he made a horror film for them first. Lebas had considered the horror project a test of his filmmaking abilities so he worked hard and did the best he could. The film was a commercial hit; everyone in Indonesia watched *The Mystery Makeup of The Ronggeng Dancer*. The film's success proved a double-edged sword for Lebas, however. The Indian head-of-production subsequently told Lebas that he should stick to making horror films. The production house refused to invest in the idealistic films Lebas wanted to make; they told him there was no money in such films, that they were a bad gamble, and a huge risk that might cause them to lose big money. After that, Lebas had been forced to settle on becoming a Class-C or at best a Class-B filmmaker.

The Indian producer had then approached him to make a sinetron, a soap opera. The production had all kinds of limitations: they had been able to shoot at only one location, and had to mostly use close-ups with a lot of voice-over to express the characters' inner thoughts. Although Lebas wanted to refuse the offer, he was out of work at the time and was desperate. The producer convinced him that it was a wonderful opportunity: 'Think of it as a challenge. Listen to me, Lebas ... Not everyone can make a soap opera. If you can rise to this challenge, then I'm sure you'll be able to make any kind of film! Now, let's talk compensation. How much money do you want? Is this enough?' He had slipped Lebas a piece of paper with a number written on it, the salary per episode he was willing to pay. Lebas could not refuse the offer.

Tegar and Karim both loved high-budget feature films as well as art-house movies, but they detested pointless horror. In their opinion, horror films didn't help Indonesian audiences progress or evolve. After Lebas's sinetron was released, Mas Tegar had commented, 'I stand corrected, Lebas. Your films aren't just preventing Indonesian audiences from progressing, they are actually setting them back a decade.'

Since then, no matter how hard Lebas tried to persuade Tegar to sponsor his films, his brother never approved of his proposals – not even when presented with a story that was filled with moral messages and featured a cast of prestigious actors.

'What do you want to propose to me now? Please don't tell me you are here to pitch another one of your ideas,' Tegar said scornfully as Lebas entered the room.

Lebas rolled his eyes, annoyed. 'I don't want to pitch anything to you. Even if I did, I would surely lose out to Ipung Wardoyo. I have come here to claim my share of the factory.'

'What do you want to do with it?'

'Make a film.'

'No!'

'Mas, I'm not submitting a proposal for an art grant to some foundation. I am only asking that my share be liquidated, so that I can use it to make a film.'

'I won't allow it!' Tegar insisted.

'Liquidating my share is my right! I also own Djagad Raja cigarettes, don't I?'

'As someone who knows this business, and as your older brother, it is only right that I give you some good advice: it is a terrible move to liquidate your assets, Lebas, for a new business that has no real scope.'

Lebas sprung from his seat and leaned into his brother angrily, looking like an insect ready to strike. 'And how exactly is its scope not real, Mas? Film is my world. If I am ready to grow and become successful, how dare you try and stop me?'

Tegar replied stubbornly, 'I don't believe you can make a good film. It will just be full of those cheesy close-ups, like in that soap opera you made.' He made his voice sound overwrought and melodramatic as he spoke the words, sounding like a character in a sinetron himself. 'If you could convince me that you would make something good, I would let you. But so far, your work has only been disappointing.'

And so, it was over. Lebas knew there was no point in arguing his case anymore.

* * *

'How strange humans are ... When we age our skin looks just like wrinkled bark,' Lebas murmured as he observed his father. Soeraja reminded him of the tree trunk Geppetto had crafted into Pinocchio. Perhaps, his father was like Pinocchio too, and his youthful spirit was still preserved somewhere beneath his wooden exterior.

The scar on Soeraja's forehead had been growing deeper ever since the stroke hit him. It hadn't looked so pronounced before. The scar was not special – nothing like Harry Potter's, which was in the shape of a lightning bolt and signalled his power – instead, Soeraja's scar was merely a simple line, with three stitches, cutting across the top of his forehead, near the front of his scalp. Soeraja had a bald spot there, since his hair hadn't grown properly from the dead skin.

Whenever anyone asked him about the scar, Soeraja said it was a souvenir from his wild youth. But Lebas didn't believe his father – for as long as he had known him, Soeraja had been disciplined, walking the straight and narrow path, and was never the wild man he claimed to be. Yet, Soeraja insisted that long ago he had fought with someone, and that person had smashed a kerosene lamp into his head when he had been unarmed.

'That is how I got the scar. Obviously, I lost the fight!' He would always end his story on a heroic note, even though he had lost.

As Lebas watched his sleeping father, he wondered what Jeng Yah looked like – did she have big hair, held in place with hairspray? Did she wear a big skirt, and did she like to spin around until it flared? What made Jeng Yah so memorable that even in the twilight of his life, Soeraja was still calling out her name? And, what even was Jeng Yah's full name?

Suddenly, his father gasped for breath in his sleep, coughing and moving his head fitfully from side to side. His eyes opened. 'Bas ...' he whispered faintly, calling out his nickname for Lebas.

Lebas moved closer to him. 'Yes, Father?'

'I have to pee. Please take me to the bathroom.'

'It's okay, if you have to pee, just pee ... Don't worry about it. You have a catheter.'

'Oh yes, I forgot.'

Soeraja looked away and seemed to strain as his urine flowed through the catheter tube. Then he looked towards Lebas once again.

'Bas ...'

'Yes, Father? What is it? Are you thirsty?'

'Yes.'

Lebas got up and fetched a bottle of water. He put a straw to his father's mouth. Soeraja took little sips. Then he gazed fondly at his son.

'You are my child, Bas ...'

'Yes, Father.'

'Even if you don't want to work in the family business, you

are still my child,' he said emphatically.

'Yes, Father.' Lebas's eyes welled up. His father's words made him want to cry, but he held back his tears.

When Lebas had first announced that he didn't want to work for their family business, Soeraja had sworn at him, and had threatened to cut him out of his will and remove his name from the list of heirs to the Djagad Raja clove cigarette fortune. On seeing his father's ruined body now, Lebas was reminded of the past, and he wished it wasn't too late. He wished he still had time to be more devoted to his family, that he still had time to be a good son to Soeraja.

'Father ...' he called. Soeraja looked at him with the same steady gaze. Lebas pressed on, somewhat afraid, 'Who is ... Jeng Yah?'

'How do you know about Jeng Yah?'

'You called her name in your sleep. Did you dream about her?'

Soeraja chuckled, as if realizing his foolishness. He spoke slowly, 'Yes, I dreamt about Jeng Yah. Does your mother know I asked for her?'

'She knows. Do you want to see her again?'

Soeraja chuckled again. 'Yes ... But don't tell your mother. She will be furious.'

'Father, where is Jeng Yah now?'

'We last met in Kudus. A long time ago, before you were born.' Kudus was the birthplace of Djagad Raja cigarettes. It was where Soeraja had spent his youth.

'Can you find Jeng Yah for me, Bas?'

'I don't know, Father. But I can try,' Lebas said. Then they were quiet for a long time.

Soeraja looked up at Lebas again. 'I'm tired.'

'Yes, Father, you should get some sleep,' Lebas agreed. Soeraja closed his eyes and drifted off into a comfortable sleep.

* * *

'Jeng Yah is in Kudus!' Lebas reported to his brothers the next day. 'Father wants me – um, *us* – to find Jeng Yah,' he blurted out impatiently. The brothers stared at each other. The three of them stood in an uneasy silence for a long time.

'Okay, then you should go to Kudus and try to find her,' Karim said eventually.

'Me?' Lebas said, reluctant. Kudus was hot and boring. All there was to do in the city was to look at the Kudus Tower and eat soto kudus, a local take on chicken soup. There was one other thing to do there: smoke kretek, or clove cigarettes.

'Bas, you are the most laidback person in the entire world. You have plenty of time to go wherever you feel like and do whatever you want to, don't you? But Mas Tegar and I have to take care of the factory.'

'Fine. I'll do it,' Lebas agreed grudgingly.

'Okay, it's decided then. You'll leave tomorrow ... Take a flight to Semarang, and then I'll ask our driver to pick you up at the airport and take you to Kudus.'

'Nah, I'll just drive.'

'What? Why?'

'I want to drive there ... After all, we don't have all the information we need about Jeng Yah, do we? Tegar still has to ask our mother about her, right?' As his brother looked on with annoyance, Lebas continued, 'I don't want to be wasting time in

Kudus, waiting around for information. Besides, I want to meet an old friend in Cirebon. I went to college with him in America. His place is on the way to Kudus.'

'Will you spend the night there?' Karim asked.

'Yeah. I'll spend the following day with him.'

Tegar's forehead wrinkled in anger. 'Are you crazy? We don't have time for that! You have to find Jeng Yah as soon as possible.'

'But it's about my film. It'll just be one day, I swear!' Lebas had already made contingency plans in case his two older brothers rejected his film proposal. He would finance part of the film with his own money, and he would approach a sponsor for the remaining, perhaps even ask his friends for help. Most of them still possessed the indie spirit in them and would be willing to work for little (or even for nothing).

'Fine, it's up to you,' Tegar sighed, reluctantly agreeing.

* * *

Lebas stuffed some clothes into his backpack, along with his toiletries and a hand towel. He also packed his camera, in case there was something interesting to take pictures of, and his iPod, so he could listen to music on the drive to Kudus.

Before he left, he woke Soeraja, kissing his hand. 'Father, I am going to look for Jeng Yah,' Lebas whispered in his ear.

'How do you know about Jeng Yah?'

'You told me about her yesterday.'

'I did?'

'Yes.'

'I have forgotten.'

'But you do want to see Jeng Yah again, don't you?'

'Yes, I do.' Soeraja fell silent, gazing at his son for a long time, and then his eyes closed again. Lebas hurried to leave.

He told his mother he was going to Kudus to take care of some factory business. She studied his face suspiciously but before she could ask any questions Karim interceded, 'Let him go, Mother ... Perhaps he has finally come to his senses after seeing how ill Father has become.'

Lebas threw all of his stuff into the backseat and started the car. He lit himself a Djagad Raja kretek. Hooking his iPod up to the car stereo he played the song that accompanied him on every road trip: the *Lucky Luke* theme song. 'I'm a poor lonesome cowboy a long, long way from home,' Lebas sang along. And he prayed he would reach his destination before he even knew it.

3

Marriage

For Idroes Moeria, it was a special day – a day different to the ones that had come before. He could now read well enough to borrow books from Pak Trisno and discuss them with him. Only last week he had returned the latest one he had taken from him on loan. The young man had been preparing ever since the dawn call to prayer had sounded and woken their town. Idroes had performed his sunrise prayers, and then his subuh prayers. His mother smiled, observing that her son had suddenly become so diligent about his worship. She knew it was because he had fallen in love. And today, she would go with him to ask for the hand of the girl he adored.

The woman had asked her son three times if he was certain about proposing to the daughter of the scribe. All three times Idroes Moeria had nodded with a steady resolve. His mother had named other girls in the village, who were pretty and also matched their economic status. She even advised that her son pray to Allah for guidance and ask for a sign from the All Powerful about who would be the best match for him. But Idroes Moeria was stubborn. He was certain that Roemaisa, the daughter of the scribe, was his jodoh, his soul mate and fated match. And so, if that was how he felt, there was only one way to determine whether or not this was indeed true: by taking a proposal to the girl's family.

When the sun was as high as a spear, Idroes Moeria and his mother arrived at the scribe's house. His wife greeted them warmly – welcoming them, ushering them in to have a seat. Idroes squirmed impatiently and couldn't remain seated. He was desperate to see Roemaisa, but she did not appear. Instead it was the scribe who walked into the room. His mother made polite small talk with the man for a few moments, but finally she said that her only son had fallen in love with the scribe's daughter. The man nodded. Idroes Moeria's heart was pounding. In his entire life, he had never felt so terrified. The scribe scrutinized Idroes, giving him a once over, and the latter felt like he was being stripped naked; he was struck suddenly with an irrational fear that he had forgotten to wear trousers. Then, the scribe called for his daughter: 'Roem! Roemaisa!'

Idroes Moeria would never forget the moment when she finally appeared from behind the curtain. She was wearing a kebaya blouse made out of delicate flowered lace and a long batik sarong with pleats that looked neat and crisp. Perhaps the girl had purposefully put on her best clothes to meet him, Idroes thought. Or else, she would have been wearing yesterday's batik, and the pleats would already be crumpled and dishevelled. For a moment, and only for just a moment, the girl smiled at him with her eyes. Then she politely responded to the scribe's call, 'Yes, Father?'

The scribe asked Roemaisa to sit down and join them in conversation. When she did, Idroes Moeria's heart beat even more erratically; this was the closest he had ever been to her. How he wanted to take her hand and hold it, but he controlled himself. There was no way he could do such a thing with the scribe watching them.

The scribe then explained to his daughter that Idroes Moeria had come to ask for her hand in marriage. On hearing this, Roemaisa blushed. She quickly bowed her head, hiding the exuberance that welled up in her heart – however, Idroes Moeria could tell how she felt; it was written so clearly in her face. Secretly, he was rejoicing too, but he was holding it all in. However, he felt his heart skip a beat when the scribe said that he was willing to accept any suitor for his daughter, no matter where he came from, as long as two requirements were met. First, the man had to be able to read and write.

'I don't want Roemaisa's husband to be less learned than she is,' the scribe explained. 'The man is the head of the family, after all. How could he lead if he is ignorant?'

The second requirement was that Roemaisa herself must want to take the man as her husband. The scribe would not force his daughter to marry anyone against her wishes. Roemaisa was the only girl in their family. Her three elder brothers were already married, and her younger brother hadn't yet entered puberty, so it was indeed her turn for marriage, and the scribe wanted what was best for his only daughter. The man's beliefs were more progressive than most other parents of the time, who preferred to choose husbands for their daughters. The scribe felt that securing a child's happiness required a different approach. He believed that his daughter should choose someone she loved as a partner, and that love was the most important foundation for a happy family.

After explaining his position, the scribe took a pencil and a piece of paper, and pushed them across the table towards Idroes Moeria.

'Write your name!' he ordered. Idroes said a prayer as he picked up the pencil, and he hoped that his handwriting would be legible. He had little confidence in himself, even though Pak Trisno had taught him to read and write. He wondered if he had been too hasty in coming here to propose to Roemaisa. He should have waited and taken more time to practice his penmanship.

The scribe inspected Idroes Moeria's chicken scratches. He nodded. Then he ordered, 'Write my daughter's name!'

Ah… Idroes Moeria had written Roemaisa's name hundreds of times ever since he had learned the alphabet. He knew he would get it right. The scribe again nodded.

'Now, write down the reason for your visit here today.'

Idroes Moeria wrote: 'I came here today to propose to Roemaisa.' This time the scribe let himself smile.

'How long have you been learning to write, son?'

'For about one month, sir,' Idroes said unsurely and with some embarrassment, not expecting such a question.

'Who is teaching you?'

'Pak Trisno.'

'The klobot cigarette seller?'

'Yes, sir, that's the one. But Pak Trisno no longer sells klobot because his holdings were seized by Japan.'

'Oh, really?' The scribe hadn't known about this, and he looked concerned.

'Yes, sir.' The scribe sighed as Idroes Moeria continued, 'And now I have become a klobot seller.'

'You mean you are a labourer?'

'I used to work as a labourer, rolling cigarettes for Pak Trisno, sir. But I am no longer one. The cigarettes I make now, I sell for myself.' The scribe looked surprised at Idroes Moeria's answer, and so Idroes explained, 'I bought the leftover tobacco the Japanese didn't take from Pak Trisno, and I used it to make klobot to sell in the market and in shops.' He reached into his trouser pocket. 'This is my klobot.' He showed them an unopened pack of Djojobojo Klobot. He had taken it there on purpose, wanting to show the scribe that he would be able to support Roemaisa and make her happy. The man smiled on seeing the chicken-scratch handwriting on the pack Idroes held. Then he turned to ask his daughter.

'Roem, do you want to give yourself to Idroes Moeria or not?'

She did not reply at first. Like a turtle that hides its head inside its shell, she simply bowed her head lower.

'Answer, Roem ... Would you like to marry him or not?'

Slowly, but Idroes Moeria could see it clearly, Roemaisa nodded her head. Then she whispered, 'I want to, Father.'

* * *

Roemaisa's parents didn't want their daughter to live in Idroes Moeria's house – which could be called modest, or, to be more accurate, barely adequate. With permission from his mother, after their simple wedding ceremony, Idroes Moeria moved into the scribe's house and the couple slept in Roemaisa's room.

On their first night together, Roemaisa confirmed Idroes Moeria's suspicions: she told him that Soedjagad had in fact come home to ask her hand in marriage. 'But Mas Djagad could not read or write.'

'Don't ever call him "Mas" in front of me! You only have one "Mas" and that's me!' Idroes scolded. Roemaisa smiled and nodded. Mas was a polite term for men that could simply mean older brother, but could also be used by a woman as a term of endearment for a man. Roemaisa understood that her husband was jealous.

The fact that Djagad had dared propose to Roemaisa made Idroes Moeria furious. He ravished his wife on their wedding night, the feelings of restrained anger erupting in a tempest of passionate lovemaking. At first they were awkward and naïve, since neither of them had touched someone of the opposite sex before, but they quickly learned to explore and pleasure each other's bodies. Idroes Moeria imagined the look on Djagad's face if he saw them making love so passionately, and he felt victorious.

After two months, one morning, Roemaisa suddenly felt sick to her stomach. She was disgusted by the sight of the freshly cooked rice placed before her on the table, and nauseated by the warm steam it was letting out, and she told her mother to it take away. It was undeniable that Roemaisa was now with child.

For his part, the knowledge that he had been able to get his wife pregnant made Idroes Moeria feel like a real man. Moreover, in the months since their wedding, the sales of Djojobojo Klobot had gone up. He felt elated and believed that God really cared for him after all. It was true, just like the old saying claimed: children did indeed bring good fortune. Idroes began working harder now. He felt it was the right time to make a label for his cigarettes. It was true that he couldn't afford to make slick packaging yet, but he had done the calculations and he did have enough money to make a simple label, and he certainly didn't mind the extra work of sticking the labels onto the packs of cigarettes, one by one.

On the night before he planned to visit the printer, Idroes Moeria sketched out the design for his label. He wanted something with colour and with typeset letters, not handwritten ones. It would certainly be much neater than Djagad's klobot, he thought, already imagining his sweet victory, and how upset Soedjagad would look on seeing Idroes Moeria's striking packs.

He also decided to put a picture of his own face, copied from his passport photo, on the label. That would make Djagad even angrier. He wanted every man who smoked his cigarettes to be able to recognize him. He wanted them to greet him in the street. How wonderful it would be to have people know who he was, even when he didn't know them, as if he were someone important. He wanted his face to be the symbol of Djojobojo Klobot. He wanted people to think that his name was Djojobojo. It would be incredible if everyone thought that …

First, he had his passport photo made by a photographer. He had borrowed one of his father-in-law's shirts to be photographed in, because he didn't own any smart clothes himself. He had to wait longer than usual for the photograph to be developed, because he wanted it to be in colour, and the photographer needed time to tint the black-and-white photograph. Finally it was ready. Bursting with pride, Idroes headed to the printer's shop. Along the way he noticed that M Town was quieter than usual, even though the weather was good – it wasn't raining, and there was not a cloud in the sky. Mount Merapi could be seen clearly, standing tall in the distance. It was a beautiful day, the perfect day for Idroes Moeria to improve his business – that was, until he arrived at the printers.

The printer's shop was closed. He looked around and knocked on the door repeatedly while calling out to the owner, but no one answered. He slowly realized that all the houses and shops around the printer's place were shuttered too. How come everything was closed? His hand was in his pocket, clutching his passport photo; he was eager to show it to the printer. He knocked on the door a little harder, but there was still no response from inside.

Then, Idroes felt the muzzle of a rifle press between his

shoulder blades, forcing him to raise his hands. He heard someone speaking to him, in an accent that was hard for him to understand: the voice ordered him to turn around slowly. When he obeyed, he saw three Japanese soldiers standing before him, their rifles aimed at his chest. His arms went limp – so limp that the passport photo that he had been clutching slipped out of his grasp, and fluttered to the ground ...

4

Djagad Raja Clove Cigarettes

Lebas had hoped to reach his destination before he knew it, but he had to admit defeat now. He was still driving. He realized that he did not really know his way around Cirebon. He tried calling Erik, his friend from college, but the latter didn't answer. It seemed that Erik's mobile was switched off. And then, suddenly, the music stopped. Surprised, Lebas checked his iPod.

'Damn!' The battery was dead. He turned on the radio and heard the brisk voice of an announcer reporting the news and weather forecast. He realized that he hadn't thought about what date it was, or even what day of the week it was, in quite a long time – that was what happened when you were a 'freelancer', which is how he preferred to think of himself. It sounded a lot better than 'unemployed'.

His mobile rang, and Erik's name appeared on the screen. He turned off the radio and cheerfully answered: 'Hey man, how are you doing? I guess you're a busy man, eh? I'm here in Cirebon, and I want to come see you ... What's your address?'

On the other end, Erik chuckled with satisfaction. He was pleased to hear that Lebas was coming over to meet him. He would never have guessed that Lebas, whom he hadn't seen since finishing school in San Francisco, would ever come to visit him in his hometown. Erik gave him the whereabouts of the Rasta

House, which is what he called his home that also doubled as his music studio.

When Lebas entered the Rasta House, he immediately plonked himself down on an old, flattened foam mattress lying in the corner.

'Man, this is so thin ... All you'd have to do is fry this mattress up, and it would be like a piece of seared tofu,' Lebas remarked, taking out a carton of Djagad Raja cigarettes from his bag and handing it to his friend. Erik grinned on receiving the familiar gift.

'Well, that's okay, man. It's so the musicians who come to my studio will focus on playing music, rather than taking a nap!' Erik said, laughing and scratching his head. A yellow, red and green knit-cap covered most of his dreadlocks, which had grown longer since they last met.

Although the same age as Lebas, Erik had been a few years his senior at school, and had been studying music. He was an eccentric individual, and Lebas sometimes found it difficult to understand his friend's way of thinking. After graduation, Erik could have lived in Jakarta if he had wanted to. With his musical ability and his fairly affluent background, he would have gone far there, but instead he preferred to live in Cirebon, a city with few opportunities for someone who wanted a career in music.

When he had first started college in San Francisco, Lebas had majored in Business, because his father had told him to. However, after a year, he had realized that it wasn't really his passion. So he had secretly switched to Filmmaking. When his father found out, he wrote Lebas out of his will, preventing Lebas from claiming his portion of the family inheritance, and no one in the house had interfered with this decision. They had all stood frozen in the face of Soeraja's wrath. His father hadn't talked to Lebas for three months after that. The young man tried as hard as he could to assuage his father, but the latter had acted as though Lebas didn't exist for him. It went on this way until the morning Soeraja was left half-paralyzed by his stroke. That fateful morning, Lebas's mother had mentioned to him that their youngest son was going to be an assistant director as part of his internship program at an indie film production company. His father had cursed and swore, and it was at that exact moment that the Angel of Death had come down to snatch away half his soul.

Eventually, he had forgiven Lebas. When he had recovered, in a stammering lisp, he had admitted that forgiveness was the only medicine that might be able to heal his condition. He realized that he had had a stroke because he had been upset with Lebas. A lawyer came over a few days later and drew up a new will at his request, and Lebas's name was reinstated.

When Lebas decided to switch his major a second time, to Music, because he felt that Filmmaking no longer suited him, he didn't tell anyone about it. It all began when he was invited to join a study group consisting of three of his American friends, who were also Music majors like Erik. They had been assigned to take the songs of a particular musician and give them new arrangements. The professor had instructed them to conduct deep research on any musician of their choice, and to understand his personality and the music he composed. Their group had chosen Bob Marley, and the research project had taken them all the way to Jamaica. At first Lebas had merely tagged along with the others, but he had returned home from the island feeling inspired by Marley and his music. He grew out dreadlocks, and then, one night, while he had been playing the guitar and singing 'Redemption Song', he decided that he wanted to be a musician. And a new course of study had thus followed, and suddenly Lebas found himself in music class with his own percussion kit. He left behind all the sets and costumes he had worked on as well as the thick manuscripts he needed to memorize for his major in Filmmaking.

He had been a Bob Marley follower for eight months, until some lice decided that his dreadlocks made a nice and cosy nest. One day, he had scratched his head and found two of the bugs underneath his fingernails: one of them jumped back onto his head, while he fiercely crushed the other with his thumbnail, its blood squirting out. Lebas had cried out in exasperation and annoyance at the bloodsuckers. In addition to all the marijuana he had been smoking, no wonder he had been feeling so stupid these days. He decided to shave his head immediately. Once bald, he had gotten rid of all his Bob Marley stuff too. Luckily, when Karim had arrived at the university for a visit, Lebas's hair had already grown back, and the only thing that was left from his Marley-wannabe phase was a poster on the walls of his tiny apartment, of the singer in his iconic pose, smoking a joint.

However, when Karim had found a complete drum set that Lebas had bought at the flea market, the latter was forced to admit that he wasn't studying in the Film department any more. Karim had become upset and hadn't known what to do when his younger brother begged him not to tell anyone. But Karim did tell Tegar, the first-born son, who then told their mother, who then told their father.

The matter ended with Soeraja making a phone call to Lebas, his voice stammering and slurring because of the stroke. 'I'm not mad this time. But if you change your major again, I will cut off your allowance, and I will not pay another cent for your college education!'

And so Lebas had struggled on, trying to finish college. Then a girl named Denise, with hair and eyes the colour of hazelnuts, had come into his life and stolen his heart. She had introduced him to Advertising, a subject that could make products and services seem enticing to consumers, and Lebas had taken some photography courses in order to impress her. He had wanted to change his major again, but when he remembered what his father had said about not paying for college – and not giving him any allowance – he knew he couldn't follow through.

He had been stuck with the Music major. For a while, he was disappointed, and he cut class all the time. His days were spent following Denise wherever she went. Even when she had class, Lebas faithfully waited by her side. But then one day she broke Lebas's heart, claiming that he was too possessive and never thought of his own future. Lebas tried to sway her by saying that he was a rich cigarette-factory owner in Indonesia and didn't really need to worry about his future. But then Denise had confessed the real reason for breaking up with him: she was seeing her professor, a married man. Furious, Lebas had locked himself at home, sulking, turning up his music as loud as he could, playing punk-rock songs by bands that supposedly worshipped Satan and whose vocalists were really just screaming and growling than singing. After that, he had gone back to school, returning to his music studies, and somehow had managed to graduate, faltering along the way.

Erik was the only one from the Jamaica trip who had stuck with Bob Marley. In addition to his Marley-like appearance and paraphernalia, he wrote songs in the singer's style too, and unbelievably, his face had started to morph so he even looked like him.

'What brings you here, man?' Erik asked in his distinctive Jamaican-accent. He addressed everyone close to him as 'man', and pronounced it as 'mon'. Lebas explained the reason for his visit and requested Erik help make his dream-film a reality. He confided that he didn't have a lot of money, so the pay would be minimal. In fact, he would be incredibly grateful to anyone who'd be ready to work for free.

Erik laughed at this. 'Man, do you think I'm stupid? There's no way you don't have any money!'

'I'm serious. My older brothers refuses to sponsor my film,' Lebas said, dejected.

Erik laughed again and grabbed Lebas by his shoulders good-naturedly. 'No problem. I can score your film. It's for our brotherhood, am I right, my man?' Lebas smiled. He knew he could always count on Erik.

As the night wore on, the Rasta House turned into a sticky flytrap for young musicians. Erik had invited his friends over, luring them with the news that Lebas had come for a visit and brought along cartons of Djagad Raja cigarettes. A few young Rastafarians played the song 'No Woman No Cry' on their guitars, and Erik sang along: 'Good times we've had and good times we've lost along the way ... In this bright future, you can't forget your past, so dry your tears, I say ...' Even Erik's voice sounded like Bob Marley's, Lebas realized with surprise.

One of the packs of Djagad Raja kretek that Lebas had brought along as a gift was already unwrapped, and the cigarettes had been split open and unrolled. The Bob Marley-ers had mixed in some marijuana with the tobacco and rolled them up again with fresh papers they had brought along specifically for this purpose. The Rasta House studio filled with smoke. The Djagad

Raja ganja cigarettes were circulated from mouth to mouth. Everything began to slow down and feel good.

Erik suddenly exclaimed, 'Hey, I just remembered that I have something for you, man!' He opened a cupboard and handed Lebas a pack of clove cigarettes.

'Why are you giving me a pack of Djagad Rajas? I have warehouses full of them.'

Erik shook his head, taking back the cigarettes that he has set in front of Lebas.

'No, no, look at them carefully. This is not a pack of Djagad Raja, Great Universe. This is Jagat Raya, Huge Cosmos!' Lebas wrinkled his forehead, not understanding what his friend meant. Then Erik pointed to the brand name written across the pack in the exact same font that Djagad Raja used. Erik was right, it said Jagat Raya! Lebas laughed, and Erik seemed pleased. 'See? I found them in some random small shop and bought them for you!'

It was no secret that the few clove cigarette brands that dominated the market were imitated by smaller manufacturers. They didn't just imitate the packaging, but also the name and flavour. Lebas was impressed with this brand because it had reproduced their company's packaging so accurately. But what about the taste? Lebas lit a Jagat Raya.

'It tastes different from Djagad Raja.'

'KW 12, yeah?' Erik replied, laughing.

Knock-off goods were usually called KW, followed by a number – the larger the number, the more obviously the imitation fell short of the original.

'Yeah,' Lebas agreed, still smoking. 'KW12.'

5
Tegar

Tegar stood at the side of the road, furious, mobile glued to his ear. He had been calling Lebas for quite some time now, but his brother wasn't picking up. Tegar had just gotten out of the shared van he had taken from Jakarta to Cirebon. The driver had offered to take him to his final destination, but Tegar preferred to get off at the central office, where people could get picked up or dropped off easily. He thought he would call Lebas to find out where he was, and then he would ask the driver to fetch his brother from wherever he was, so they could stay together at the hotel. Tegar was aware that on a weekend like this, it would be difficult to get a room. But he had been trying to reach Lebas for more than half an hour now, and his brother wasn't answering his phone. The minivan carrying passengers into the city had filled up and just pulled out, but was already stuck in a line of traffic right in front of Tegar – the driver who had offered him a ride nodded in a friendly manner. He tried to smile back, while calling Lebas again.

Half an hour later, an empty taxi haltingly jerked its way out of the traffic. Tegar was seated inside it, inhaling the musty smell of the vehicle's interior mixed with the sour body odour of the driver, who probably hadn't changed his uniform in days. Tegar asked the driver to take him to a hotel, any hotel, as long as it had a room available. Perhaps he was stupid, or perhaps he was doing it on purpose so he'd earn a higher fare, but the driver was taking Tegar to Jalan Cipto, the busiest road in all of Cirebon, especially on the weekends.

When he arrived at the hotel, Tegar once again tried to contact his little brother, but still couldn't get through to him. He wasn't worried something bad might have happened to Lebas. Instead, Tegar was feeling furious, his anger rising from his toes and rushing up to the crown of his head. He knew his little brother did whatever he felt like doing, without any concern for others. Maybe he was partying at a nightclub and had left behind his mobile at the hotel on purpose. It was indeed a good decision that he had decided to catch up with Lebas. If he hadn't, then his brother would surely have abandoned the Jeng Yah business and run off to have more fun. Tegar gave up trying to contact Lebas and decided to get some sleep in order to calm himself.

The next morning, he tried calling Lebas again. This time his brother picked up. It was obvious that he had just woken up. His sleepy voice said hello at the other end.

'Where are you? Why aren't you picking up your phone? I've been looking for you all night ... I'm here in Cirebon!'

'What? Why? Did Father die?' Lebas blurted out in alarm.

'*Did Father die*? Did Father die? Man! You're the kind of guy who wouldn't think twice about cursing his own parents, or wishing they were dead, huh? You don't care about anyone else but yourself. It makes sense, then, that you didn't pick up the phone. What were you doing last night?'

'I was hanging out with my friends ...'

'Which hotel are you staying at now? I'm coming there now!'

'Mas, I'm not at a hotel. I spent the night at my friend's music studio.'

'So, where did you sleep?'

'I slept here. There is enough place to sleep here.'

'Lord have mercy. Bas, you are too old to be living so carelessly.' Tegar could never stop worrying about his little brother and his happy-go-lucky lifestyle. If Lebas hadn't been part of the Soeraja family and a co-owner of the Djagad Raja Clove Cigarette Factory, he would have had no future. Tegar was certain of this. He decided to go and pick up his little brother, even though he didn't know where the Rasta House was located. Lebas handed his mobile to Erik, who gave the directions in his unique blend of Indonesian and Bob Marley slang. Tegar struggled to understand what he was saying, but was determined to go anyway. That was a better option than having to wait for Lebas to come to him – three days could pass, and his younger brother still wouldn't have shown up at the hotel.

When Tegar arrived, he found that Lebas hasn't showered. His brother looked scruffy and dishevelled, and was still lying on a mattress in a corner of the studio. He sniffed at his brother's clothes.

'You've been smoking, haven't you?' he asked like a policeman interrogating a criminal.

'Of course. So what? You know I smoke.'

'I mean you've been smoking marijuana, haven't you?'

Lebas didn't respond, and Tegar took his silence to mean assent. 'Clean yourself up! Change your clothes! We are going to Kudus.'

'*We*?'

'Yes, we!'

* * *

Lebas was in the passenger seat. He wasn't allowed to drive. Tegar wasn't sure his little brother had completely sobered up yet. He had instructed Lebas to leave all his belongings at the Rasta House; if they did come across any policemen on the way, he didn't want them to catch the scent of marijuana in their car. If they did, then the brothers would find themselves trying to 'check out of a free hotel' – or, in other words, trying to get out of prison.

Before leaving the city, Tegar stopped at a car wash. He promised the cleaners a nice tip if they vacuumed the whole car. After that, he stopped by a clothing store to buy Lebas some new clothes, right down to fresh underwear.

'But I really like my old jacket!' Lebas complained as they got back in the car. He was disgruntled that he had been forced to leave behind his wrinkled denim jacket at the Rasta House.

'You are a grown up. Stop acting like a big baby,' Tegar scolded. 'I should have stopped holding your hand a long time ago. I refuse to take care of you anymore.'

'I never asked for you to take care of me.'

'You're a kid who doesn't know how lucky he is!'

'I'm not a kid,' Lebas countered, sounding annoyed.

'Well, if you're not a kid, then start acting like an adult!' Tegar shouted.

Suddenly Lebas chuckled at him.

'Don't you realize you're being scolded? Why are you laughing!' the elder brother demanded angrily.

'Because you nag like an old lady. You're starting to sound just like Mother.'

Tegar looked away, refusing to meet his brother's eyes. Lebas had successfully made him shut his mouth. He started the car again, instructing his younger brother to put on his seatbelt.

Tegar couldn't help himself. He had always taken life seriously, ever since he was little. When he was still only a child, Soeraja had started taking him to the factory, teaching him how to roll cigarettes, and how to monitor the workers, and even how to smoke. Think about it: has any other parent ever taught their child to smoke? His father had prepared a sample of different brands of cigarettes and asked him to try them, and to pay attention to their taste. Tegar's tongue had been trained from that young age to tell which cigarettes were tasty and which weren't, and eventually he had been taught that the most savoury and delicious cigarette in the world was a Djagad Raja clove and that the other brands didn't even come close to it.

Back then, the Soeraja family was still living in Kudus. Tegar had just shown his mother his middle-school report card when his father had called him into his office and instructed him to try one of the clove cigarettes he had rolled himself. Tegar had stood frozen, staring at the pack of cigarettes. Father had nudged a cigarette out of the pack, and told his son, who wasn't even sixteen years old then, to pull it out and light it. He had been nervous and uncomfortable, but his father had given him a reassuring nod, and then the cigarette was in Tegar's hand. Soeraja had taken one for himself too; he had clicked the lighter and sucked on the cigarette, and smoke had came out of his mouth and nose. Tegar had watched him carefully. Then his father clicked the lighter again and handed it to him. He had hesitated for a moment, but then he lit his cigarette. He inhaled it. Kretek-kretek, he could still hear the sound of the cloves burning and crackling at the tip of the cigarette. When he had coughed, Soeraja had laughed and patted his son on the back affectionately. 'Finish it!' he had said. 'I rolled it myself, especially for you.' Tegar had tried to enjoy the cigarette. Even though his friends had already started experimenting with cigarettes, he had never done so himself. Sometimes his school friends would ask him to bring them a few cigarettes from the factory, and Tegar would oblige out of friendship, and only because he knew it would never be noticed if he stole four or five from a freshly rolled batch.

Although firstborn Tegar had always known he would be burdened with the management of the Soeraja family cigarette factory, he hadn't thought it would start so soon. In his heart, he had wanted to experience all the things boys his age did, like stealing stray cigarettes from his father, and being scared of getting discovered, then smoking out back behind the school, in the open air, where the smell of burnt tobacco would fade before the teachers could sniff it out. He certainly hadn't wanted his own father to roll, offer and even light the cigarette for him, and then demand that he finish it.

'Do you know how lucky you are, Gar?' Soeraja had asked through the puffs of smoke. His face had looked very serious. 'If you wanted, you could smoke until you were lightheaded every single day. Other people have to work in order to be able to buy good cigarettes. But not you.' Tegar had stayed silent, listening to Father. He had been aware even then that he was being instructed and groomed. Perhaps, because he had graduated middle school, his father had thought of him as already grown up. 'Later, once you have graduated college, you won't need to worry about finding a job. All you have to do is watch over our factory. Other people have to go out searching for work, and once they find a job, they would be paid peanuts – the point is, your life will be quite comfortable, and all you have to do is take good care of our business.'

When he had graduated high school, the big family secret had been revealed to Tegar: he had been given the recipe for the sauce used in their cigarettes, which was completely exclusive to their Djagad Raja brand, as was the exact proportion of tobacco and cloves used. The sauce was the key ingredient that differentiated the taste of one brand of clove cigarette, or kretek, from another. The sauce was the lifeblood of a cigarette factory, and only Tegar was made privy to it. Lebas and Karim weren't given the Djagad Raja secret recipe. Their father had sworn Tegar to confidentiality and made him promise he would not reveal the sauce to anyone, including his own brothers; Tegar had in turn duly taken a binding oath and signed and sealed a formal contract with Soeraja, assuring he would never leak the recipe. Even Lebas and Karim knew about this. The sauce had to be guarded as closely as the secret of the mixture of ingredients, and Tegar kept his promise. Although he was the type of person who could easily get carried away when he talked and usually let the cat out of the bag when he opened his mouth, he had always been cautious not to mention the sauce to anyone..

Tegar could never define exactly what 'savoury' meant. To him, savoury was a perfect combination of salty and sweet, and a result of not merely two ingredients – salt and sugar – but from other flavours as well, and it made you just a little thirsty. But his father's version of savoury was different. To Soeraja, savoury was a taste that made people feel so satisfied they didn't want to try anything else, and were persuaded to return again and again to the same familiar taste. According to Tegar, his father's way of thinking seemed extremely commercial.

Once the recipe for the sauce had been handed to him, Soeraja had taken his son on a tour around the factory. This had been a little strange because Tegar had fully and thoroughly explored every corner of the place already; he had played there as a child, and he knew its every corridor and corner, and he even knew how many ghosts lived under the tamarind tree where the employees rested their fixed-gear onthel bicycles. Then, his father had introduced Tegar to the company's employees, one by one, from the managerial staff to the giling workers, whose job it was to roll the cigarettes, and the bathil workers, whose job it was to neaten and trim their edges. This felt all the more ridiculous, because they had all seen Tegar so often amongst them, and he already knew so many of them.

'So we meet again, eh, Gar? You forgot my name, huh?' one of the workers had teased him in Javanese. His father had just smiled, and Tegar hadn't said anything in return.

'One day, Gar, you are going to be responsible for all these people. You will have to be able to sell cigarettes in order to pay their salaries. You will have to provide them with healthcare benefits and you will have to be able to pay their holiday bonus every year, which means that you will double their usual salary. These people will be your responsibility, Gar, along with their wives or their husbands and their children.' Tegar's heart had sunk low when he had realized that a large burden was being transferred onto his small shoulders. 'If this factory fails, these people will be without work, and they won't be able to eat. They won't be able to send their children to school, and they will fall into poverty. Do you want something like that to happen?' Soeraja had asked.

For the entire duration of the month-long vacation before the new school year began, his father had made Tegar work as a roller in the factory. Rolling cigarettes was nothing new for the boy.

Ever since childhood, he had helped out, idly rolling the kretek in the midst of playing around the factory. Even though the rolling was usually done by women, Tegar had felt comfortable in their company. During the time spent working at the factory, Tegar had come to the conclusion that the rollers' hands possessed minds of their own. He observed that while the women were busy gossiping and bantering, their nimble hands worked continuously, like machines that had been programmed to do only that. Mbok Marem, or Mrs Marem, one of the senior rollers in the factory, had taught Tegar to roll cigarettes properly. She smiled easily, and her body was endowed with the generous curves typical of Javanese women. Sometimes he also had joined in trimming and packing the cigarettes that had been rolled, which was usually done by men.

However, Tegar had been hoping to play and have fun during his annual vacations like the other children, and like his two younger brothers, Karim and Lebas, who were free to do whatever they wanted. It wasn't easy for a boy his age to stay at the factory and work; what made it worse was Lebas's childish behaviour, because he teased Tegar every chance he got and bragged about how he had just been playing this game or that, or how he had been hanging out with his friends. As a result, Tegar secretly became quite resentful and frustrated, but he had no intention of letting his little brothers, or anyone else, know about how he felt.

Soon Soeraja had asked for his firstborn to follow the workday hours of his employees. He was even to be paid like the other workers. Tegar, the responsible teenager, would have no more vacations. He only left the factory after he had registered to begin high school. Once, when his friends had invited him to go to Kudus Tower, he had asked his father for permission to take the day off, but his father had refused. Tegar had protested that his holiday was being ruined by Soeraja, but his father had said in response, 'Why do you want to go to Kudus Tower? You've been there so many times. Are you going to see anything new there? It hasn't changed. It's still exactly the same as it always is. If you want to go somewhere and have fun, it would be better if you invited all our factory workers on a group excursion, so they could also experience the pleasure of some leisure time after all their hard work.' Tegar had been at a loss for words on hearing this – once his father had mentioned the workers, it was as if the weight placed upon his small shoulders had grown heavier. Even on Sundays, Soeraja had kept him busy, teaching him how to manage the factory. He had invited the factory treasurer over to teach Tegar about the monthly expenses that were to be paid, as well as about the income earned. The man had brought along a pile of accounting books with him. Tegar was left dumbfounded by the numbers.

'Mas Tegar is going to take Mr Raja's place, is that it?' asked Mbok Marem. She had been rolling cigarettes for Soeraja ever since Djagad Raja had been founded – long before the name 'Great Universe' was used for their brand, and when the cigarette factory had still been owned by Tegar's grandfather. Mbok Marem was older than their father.

'Of course. Who else, if not Mas Tegar?' another worker, who looked to be about as old as Mbok Marem's children, answered in Javanese. 'You're very determined, aren't you, Mas Tegar? If that's how it is, I will be loyal to you,' Marem had assured him. Her words made the weight on Tegar's back grow even heavier.

On the weekends, his father had taken Tegar to Temanggung, the place where he purchased tobacco and cloves for their factory.

They once stopped by a village called Legoksari, where it was rumoured that the fields had been struck by a falling star only a few weeks ago. Being struck by a falling star sounded like a farfetched thing indeed, but the villagers believed that if one did land on a tobacco field, srinthil would grow there abundantly. Srinthil was tobacco with the highest levels of nicotine, which of course was sold at the highest price – the very best could fetch up to 700,000 rupiah per kilogram, depending on its quality. The sale of such tobacco would bring exponential profits.

After that, they continued their journey to the ordinary tobacco fields, where the tobacco was of good quality but not as good as srinthil. As soon as their car pulled up, a thin man named Pak Muri rushed over to greet them.

'This is Tegar, my oldest son. He will take my place at the company one day,' said Soeraja without hesitation. 'And Tegar, this is Pak Muri,' he introduced. The man immediately assumed a friendly and respectful demeanour towards Tegar, knowing that this responsible kid would one day be his boss and in charge of selecting the tobacco and cloves. They walked past fields of tobacco that stretched out towards the horizon. On their perimeter, the leaves that had already been picked were laid out in the sun. All of the workers looked filthy. Smears of tobacco stuck to their clothes, leaving behind brown stains that could not be washed away even after being laundered over and over, and the smell of their bodies was nauseating. But Soeraja called it the scent of money.

Pak Muri walked them past a number of bamboo storehouses. He would occasionally stop to greet the people buying tobacco from his employees. They soon entered a storehouse that only had a few buyers inside. One of them, a middle-aged man, greeted

Soeraja, and they were quite friendly with each other. Tegar could guess that the man was also a regular buyer of Pak Muri's tobacco. As soon as his father introduced the man to him, Tegar forgot his name, but he noted the pack of cloves he took out of his pocket: Four Bracelets. Perhaps he was the owner of the brand ...

'So, you are to be the successor of Great Universe cigarettes, eh? I have to watch out for you then. You will be my competitor, after all,' Mr Four Bracelets joked. Tegar shook his hand with a small smile.

Soeraja had grabbed a handful of chopped tobacco from a small one-kilogram bundle that was bound and placed in a large basket, along with fifty or sixty more such bundles. He had inhaled the aroma of the tobacco, felt its texture in his hand and examined its colour. Then he had given Tegar a bit of it, and Tegar had done everything his father had, even though he didn't really understand anything yet about choosing the best kind of tobacco. Then, his father had put a fistful of the tobacco into a brown envelope and labelled it with the number of the basket and bundle the tobacco belonged to. In the same fashion, his father had selected tobacco from a number of other baskets. He and Pak Muri were soon haggling, and then finally had shaken hands.

Soeraja, Tegar, Mr Four Bracelets and Pak Muri had then walked out of the storehouse. They passed another building that was even quieter. A Chinese buyer was haggling with a fat employee, but there was no one else inside. His father called the fat man over. They greeted each other and chatted for a while. Tegar tugged on his father's shirt to ask, 'If this storehouse is less crowded, why didn't we just buy the tobacco here, Father?' Soeraja had gestured for him to be quiet and proceeded to continue his friendly conversation with the fat man.

The group then sat down on wooden pallets to chat. Some of the workers were already relaxing there: drinking coffee, eating fried bananas and smoking cigarettes. Tegar could not bear to sit still while looking out at the tobacco fields spread green before him. His father had given him permission to explore them and, wasting no time, Tegar immediately ran in between the rows of tobacco. He inhaled the fresh air of the fields and the aroma of the leaves, which seemed to lift him off the ground, and he closed his eyes, letting the sun caress his eyelids, and he thought, I am flying, and the tobacco leaves are my wings. The workers were still busy picking, and they had watched Tegar and smiled. A few of them cautioned him not to trip on the uneven ground but he knew he would not stumble; he was flying after all. It was at that exact moment that Tegar realized he had fallen in love with tobacco.

On returning home from Temanggung, he had asked his father again, 'Why didn't we buy our tobacco from the quieter storehouse?'

This time, Soeraja responded. 'Did you see that Chinese man? He owns the cigarette brand 999, and he always buys from that storehouse, which sells top-notch tobacco. If I bought our tobacco there, we would have to raise the price of our cigarettes, and if we raised the price of our cigarettes, our customers would probably move on to another brand, because ours would have become too expensive for them. Which would mean that our kretek might not sell at all. And if they don't sell, then I can't pay my employees. Do you understand?'

Tegar understood, but he didn't say anything.

'One day, you will be the one who has to make these decisions and strategize on making our cigarettes sell. One day, hopefully, you will be able to buy the tobacco in that storehouse, and you will be the one waited on by the owner of the tobacco plantation. Yes?'

Tegar remained quiet, mulling over his father's words. Soeraja had been able to guess what his son was doing and had offered him a Djagad Raja clove.

'If you want to think something over, it is best to do so while smoking.' Tegar had taken the cigarette and lit it, and had relished the savoury taste of the Great Universe clove as it filled the inside of his mouth.

The 999 brand of kretek was the leading make of clove cigarettes at the time, with their packs of red and gold. His father had told him that the brand had existed long before Djagad Raja – they had been doing business since before Independence, when the Dutch had still occupied the land, and had been around when the years still had started with the numbers 18 rather than 19. So, it was no surprise that 999 was already a large business and a well-established brand. They often advertised their product in magazines and newspapers, and sometimes used a picture of a dashing gentleman smoking one of their cigarettes, a priyayi man with high-class ancestry.

Djagad Raja also advertised in the newspapers. Their adverts were not very large and there were not too many of them, but there were enough to introduce their cigarettes to potential customers. Djagad Raja cloves became well known largely from word-of-mouth publicity. Tegar vowed that one day he would print full-page Djagad Raja advertisements in newspapers *and* magazines, and he would create ones that would stand out and were different from those made by other cigarette brands, so people would know that theirs was the number one kretek in the market. Moreover, he would make sure people knew about Djagad Raja as a patron of great arts events. Tegar realized that his father was right: smoking cigarettes could help one think clearly and give one a fresh perspective. It felt like the smoke was carrying him to the clouds, and he was flying amongst them ... The smoke was inspiring him to envision what Djagad Raja could become in the future, and what their company could achieve. After his last drag, Tegar had dozed off and remained asleep until they had returned home to Kudus.

* * *

Tegar glanced at Lebas. His brother was nodding off in the passenger's seat. While asleep, Lebas did not look annoying; rather, he seemed like a good child who would follow his family's advice. But what could be done with him? Lebas refused to listen to their father, let alone obey Tegar who was only his older brother. A moment later, Lebas stretched, opening his sleepy eyes and yawning wide. Tegar reached to cover his brother's mouth.

'Shut your mouth when you yawn ... Your breath stinks!' he scolded. But in a move typical of Lebas, his brother opened his mouth wider instead, and leaned in close to Tegar's face and exhaled forcefully. Then he laughed.

'Ah, damn you! I'm driving!'

Lebas laughed harder. 'I'm still sleepy ... I didn't get enough sleep.'

'How could you possibly get enough sleep the way you live? If you keep up like this, Bas, your body will be ruined before you are an old man.'

'Yeah, yeah ... nag, nag.'

The brothers fell silent for a moment. Then, unexpectedly,

Tegar asked an unusual question: 'So, I hear you are making another film?'

Lebas looked at his elder brother in astonishment, unable to believe that he wanted to discuss his film project. 'Yeah, I am! But it isn't going to be a horror film ... It's going to be a really awesome film. I have the screenplay with me,' he said enthusiastically, reaching for his bag in the backseat and sliding out the laptop he had brought along. Lebas carried it with him wherever he went. 'Here, it is ... I wrote it myself. Or, do you want to read the treatment instead? I gave my copy to Mas Karim, so I don't have it with me right now. If you want, I could print another one for you.'

'Oh my god, enough! Just close it! I won't be able to read it now anyway.' Tegar was trying to focus on his driving. Lebas's face fell, and he closed his computer with a long sigh.

The truth was that Tegar didn't want to sully the reputation of Djagad Raja cigarettes by sponsoring bad films. Moreover, as far as he could determine from his research, producing a film could be a meticulous and hair-splitting business. The sponsor had to pay attention to the process of making and releasing the movie, because it often wasn't clear for what purpose all the billions of rupiah spent were being used; there were lots of ways in which the money could be misused or embezzled. Tegar had seen his little brother's previous work, and he was sure that he hadn't seen anything on the level of the other art that Djagad Raja had sponsored so far. Even though Lebas was his brother, sponsorship was still part of their family business, and Tegar didn't want to lose his investment. Even if he wasn't going to earn profits on the investment, at the very least he wanted to make sure Djagad Raja was sponsoring something prestigious and capable of elevating the company's good name. So it wasn't just a matter of providing financial assistance to his beloved little brother, but the decision also involved taking into consideration their business's reputation and public relations. This was something Lebas didn't understand.

They drove on in silence. Tegar knew that Lebas was hurt. He tried to change the topic, saying, 'I asked Mother about Jeng Yah.'

'What? You did? Seriously?' Lebas said, shocked.

'Yeah, seriously. That's why I decided to follow you to Cirebon. And that is why I kept trying to call you so many times last night. I wanted to tell you about it.'

'And?'

'You know the scar that our father has on his forehead?'

'Yes, why?'

'You remember what he told us about it?'

'He said he fought with someone when he was young.'

'Well, he was lying to us. That is no ordinary scar. He got it when Jeng Yah whacked him on the head with a kerosene lamp.'

'What?'

'Yeah, and also, Jeng Yah struck him with that lamp on our parents' wedding day!'

'What?' Lebas gaped at him in disbelief. Tegar nodded, proud that he had been able to extract such shocking truth from their mother.

'She punched him after the couple recited their marriage contract. Father ended up looking horrible in their wedding photos.'

'No wonder Mother was so mad at Jeng Yah. But why would Father want to see Jeng Yah after she punched him in the face?' Lebas wondered.

'Maybe he owes her something.'

'What could he possibly owe her?'

'How should I know? The point is, we are going to look for Jeng Yah so we can find out why our father wants to see her again.'

The brothers grew silent once again, lost in their own thoughts, both imagining how angry someone would have to be for them to dare interrupt a wedding and then, in front of everyone, take a kerosene lamp, with its metal base and glass canister, and smash it into the bridegroom's forehead.

6

Roemaisa

Night had fallen, but Idroes Moeria still hadn't come home. Roemaisa was waiting anxiously for him. She had cooked her husband's lunch earlier that day, and the food had been lying cold for hours. Even though her mother had been asking her to eat, reminding her that the baby growing inside her needed nutrition, Roemaisa wouldn't listen. Since the afternoon and early evening, she had been stubbornly waiting for her husband to return. But Idroes didn't appear, and the day had taken a bleak turn. Now Roemaisa's parents acknowledged that they truly had a reason to worry. The scribe decided to go out and look for his son-in-law.

That night, the air in M Town seemed suddenly eerie and tense. Most of the houses were blanketed in darkness, their kerosene lamps left unlit. The eyes of wild cats glowed fiercely in the darkness, and the cries of the nocturnal creatures intensified, as if announcing bad news. There was the occasional soft thud of a mango or rose apple falling from the trees, a repast not yet eaten by the greedy fruit bats. The scribe returned home empty-handed, and Roemaisa burst into tears: her husband was missing. During his search, the scribe had heard that a number of young men had been rounded up by the Japanese and forcibly taken to Soerabaia. That was all he could tell his distraught daughter.

The next day, a kid came running from the market, carrying a coloured passport photo with Idroes Moeria's face on it. 'I found it in front of the printer's house, Miss,' he informed Roemaisa.

'I must speak with the printer! Take me there!' she demanded. But the child did not budge. 'Let's go, quickly! What are you waiting for?' Roemaisa asked frantically.

'Um, I don't know, Miss,' the kid mumbled nervously, 'It's just that ... The Japanese captured the printer and took him to Soerabaia. So perhaps, it's possible ... that Mas Idroes was also ...' Roemaisa broke down into sobs, afraid she had become a widow.

* * *

Nobody knew what happened to the men who had been taken by the Japanese. It was rumoured that once they had reached Soerabaia, they were sent to a place called Koblen. What was Koblen? Nobody knew. Roemaisa was truly panic-stricken. She wanted to go out and look for Idroes Moeria, but her parents asked her to hide instead, because they had heard that the Japanese were also taking female captives to be used as comfort women. She grew depressed. She did nothing but cry all day long, until her vision blurred and her eyes became swollen. She didn't eat or drink; the only thing she tasted for days was the salt of her own tears, and soon even they were drying up. The occasional sob still came, but not one more teardrop fell from her eyes. Roemaisa's body had grown thin in just a few days, and her skin had wrinkled up, as if she had aged ten years, and her hair had fallen out. All of her body's nutrition was being taken by the baby, and her beauty was being destroyed by grief. Finally there was no nutrition left for the little one either, so it decided to leave Roemaisa's womb.

When the scribe and his wife asked Mak Iti', the midwife who took care of the pregnant women in M Town, to come check on Roemaisa, they were informed that the child was already dead inside. The examination ended with Mak Iti' taking the foetus out of the young woman's womb. Even as the remains of the baby were taken out of her body, Roemaisa remained detached and unmoved. Her mother was overcome with sadness, unable to bear seeing her only daughter suffer so.

* * *

Idroes Moeria had been gone for a year. The people in M Town were struggling to survive; the city had become a dismal and bleak place for them. The scribe had no more work. He had been suspected of being a spy, because he had often worked with the Dutch, but luckily he had been able to hide from the Japanese raids. He had been forced to take shelter in a bunker with a number of Indonesian freedom-fighters for weeks. His wife was left alone to care for Roemaisa, who was still depressed. She was a strong woman – if she hadn't been, the depression would have claimed her too.

When the city folk heard the news that the Japanese did not think M Town was strategically important and that they would be leaving their city soon, they began to cheer up and things appeared to improve. The scribe returned home. Everyone began to clean up their houses, and once again lit their kerosene lamps when night fell. A few tradeswomen in the market dared to reopen their stalls, although they were forced to sell their goods at very high prices because everything was still so scarce. The scribe and his wife finally opened the door to the room where Roemaisa was hiding. The mother bathed her pale and listless daughter in warm water, all the while whispering prayers that she should return to her healthy and beautiful self, even though she no longer had a husband.

'I will wait for Mas Idroes.' These were the first words Roemaisa had spoken in months.

Her parents brought her outside and sat her down on the verandah, and she felt the warmth of the sun on her skin after such a long time. As her mother swept clean the compound's yard, Roemaisa's gaze fell on some piles of cornhusks that had been laid out in the sun. They had been dried and kept ready to be cut and rolled into cigarettes, but had been sitting in forgotten stacks for a long time because no one had tended to them. She stood up and went inside, while her parents looked on in confusion. She went looking for her husband's unsold klobot. When she found the stash, Roemaisa took one of the cigarettes, lit it with a match, and inhaled deeply. The cigarette had been stored for so long, and its aroma and taste were far from fresh, but she didn't care.

At first the scribe was upset, and wanted to forbid it, but his wife silenced him.

'Leave her be. Let our daughter exhale away all her sadness ... Let it blow away in the wind like smoke.'

* * *

It was as if every mouthful of klobot smoke Roemaisa inhaled reinvigorated her. The sorrows that had piled up inside her seemed to evaporate with every exhalation of smoke from her mouth. Slowly, but surely, Roemaisa recovered. However, she could not return to the old Roemaisa she had once been, so feminine and obedient. The new Roemaisa was feisty. She gathered cornhusks to lay out in the sun, and she learned how to roll a mixture of tobacco and cloves. She packed every ten cigarettes together and wrote 'Djojobojo Klobot' on each pack. Her handwriting was much better than that of her husband. She sold the cigarettes in the market and shops, and every two days, she collected the money from the sales.

Roemaisa's mother decided to sell her golden necklace and bracelets to buy chopped tobacco and cloves for her daughter. The scribe did not approve of this; he believed that his daughter's actions only proved she was still consumed with grief. He preferred the other Roemaisa, the daughter who was agreeable and obedient, who bowed her head when spoken to, and who served others like a good Javanese girl. But his wife said to him, 'That Roem doesn't exist anymore. Who will you accept: the Roem who is living with us now? Or the Roem of a month ago who was here yet still as good as gone, as if she were already dead?'

The scribe knew his wife was right. Besides, he had been without work ever since the Dutch left and the Japanese had taken their place. He was living off his savings, but felt extremely lucky that he hadn't been one of the men dragged off to Soerabaia by the Japanese.

Roemaisa was no longer a young girl, and had been marked a widow. Everyone in M Town was sure that Idroes Moeria had died in Soerabaia, even though there had been no word of his death, or any news of him at all. The men competed with one another to take his place; there was even more interest in her now than before she was married, because the new Roemaisa was not as docile as she had been then. This new woman was commanding and independent. She was struggling to rise after sinking for so long, and this made men want to offer their hand, to pull her into their embrace. But Roemaisa remained unmoved. All she cared about was her husband's cigarette business and nothing else.

Idroes Moeria's passport photo had become an invaluable keepsake for Roemaisa. She framed it and placed it in her room. When it was bedtime, she would hold it for comfort. Her mother would find her sleeping with the photograph still clutched in her hand, and could see the teardrops still clinging to the corner of Roemaisa's eyes. But the next morning, Roemaisa never looked sad. She would go back to taking care of her husband's klobot business, as if there was nothing more important in this world for her to do.

One man pursued Roemaisa most aggressively. It was none other than Soedjagad, who was lucky he hadn't been taken to Soerabaia. Full of confidence, he approached Roemaisa and spoke to her frankly of his affections. He even offered to give her some extra money to develop the Djojobojo Klobot brand, but she always refused. Then one day, Soedjagad came over to her house and told the scribe that he intended to propose to Roemaisa.

'I know how to read and write now, sir, if that is still a requirement.'

'That's no longer the issue. The situation is different now, Gad. My daughter is not really mine to give anymore.'

'Not really yours? How exactly, sir? She's still your child, isn't she? She still lives in your house. It's true that she was married, but now she's single. She's a widow.'

Before the scribe had the chance to respond to Soedjagad, Roemaisa burst out from behind the curtain. 'I am not a widow!' she said fiercely. 'We still don't know whether my husband is alive or dead. And as long as we don't know for sure, I will wait for Mas Idroes. Now, you'd better leave before I lose my respect for you ... for your rude and presumptuous behaviour!'

Soedjagad immediately excused himself.

One week passed, and then two weeks, and Djagad didn't dare show his face to her. Even when he saw Roemaisa in the market collecting her payments, he avoided her. But then one day he tracked her down and asked for her forgiveness. She forgave him and after that Soedjagad once again grew bold and tenacious in his desire for Roemaisa. He would ask her out to drink cendol with him, and he would escort her home after they had their fill of the coconut milk sweetened with palm sugar. So, even though she had already refused him, people began to think that Roemaisa and Soedjagad were getting close to each other. Word spread that there would be a merger between Djojobojo and Djagad cigarettes soon.

'What does that mean?' Roem wondered to herself when she overheard a tradeswomen repeating this rumour at the market.

'It's true, don't you know? Miss Roem must be waiting for the right time to marry Mas Djagad. He himself said it was only a matter of determining an auspicious date for their wedding. Hey, here he is now.'

Soedjagad walked into the market with a radiant face, but Roemaisa was enraged. He was caught off guard when, before he had the chance to speak even a word, Roemaisa shoved him with all her might, so forcefully that he fell backwards to the ground.

'Don't come near me ever again! I am *not* available!'

The incident became a hot topic of conversation for the city folk. Roemaisa had landed a devastating bomb on Soedjagad's self-respect. But that was nothing compared to the two bombs that America soon dropped on two Japanese cities. People began to discuss it everywhere – in the street and in the market, and when they went to call on one another. They discussed it not just to exchange news but also to be sure they knew more about the topic than their neighbours did.

In houses across the city, similar conversations could be heard:

'What is the name of the city that got bombed?'

'One of them is Nogosari. I have forgotten the other one.'

'Huh, Nogosari ... Doesn't that sound like the name of a dish?'

'Well, that's what it's called.'

They gathered in those houses that had concealed radio sets, which had been outlawed during the entire Japanese occupation and which were now rare possessions. At ten o'clock on the morning of Friday 17 August 1945 they listened to a special broadcast. Soekarno and Hatta, who were members of the Committee to Prepare for Indonesian Independence, announced their resounding Proclamation of Indonesian Independence in Jakarta: Indonesia was free.

Then, miraculously, one by one, the men who had been taken from Indonesia for forced labour began to return. They seemed to materialize out of the morning fog. They came looking like living corpses, but as the city folk squinted and looked harder, they could clearly recognize the citizens of M Town who had gone missing almost two years ago. They were skinny, filthy and beaten down, yet their eyes still held a persistent glimmer of hope. Roemaisa held onto to an anxious hope as well. She went to call on the men who had returned home, asking them if they had any news of Idroes Moeria. There were some who said they had seen him in Koblen when he had first arrived, but they all warned her that anyone who entered that place came out changed. 'Don't be surprised if you don't recognize him anymore. And remember, he might have lost his body and soul there – perhaps he even gave up and decided to die, or perhaps he was killed.'

One month after the declaration, Idroes Moeria walked in through the front door. Roemaisa greeted him with never-ending embraces and tears. It was true, as the men had warned her, that Idroes Moeria had changed. She almost didn't recognize her own husband – he was not the man she remembered, his face no longer resembled the image in the passport photograph, which had become etched in her mind during his absence. Idroes Moeria never spoke about what he had experienced in Soerabaia. He preferred to rebuild the life he had left behind in M Town.

The people at the market were surprised at Idroes Moeria's return. They shook his hand and greeted him like a hero when he arrived there with his wife. Djagad and his helper, who were distributing their klobot, watched the couple from a distance.

'It's true ... Miss Roem is not a widow. Djagad went too far!'

'Too far? How exactly, Ma'am?' Idroes Moeria asked one of the market women when he overheard their gossip.

'Your woman didn't tell you? Djagad proposed to Roemaisa while you were away, claiming that she was a widow. But she kept turning him down.'

Idroes Moeria was furious. He felt rage pulse through his body, rising up from the tips of his toes to the crown of his head. His hands clenched into fists, and he went to find Soedjagad, the man who had disrespected him and his wife. Not even Roemaisa could restrain her husband's anger, although she tried to calm him by saying that she had already chastised Soedjagad herself.

Idroes Moeria found Djagad and with all of his strength, and all of the anger and frustration he had been forced to endure when held captive in Koblen, he landed a punch on his rival's face. The entire marketplace turned to watch, but it was over in an instant. Djagad fell headfirst to the ground with a bloody nose. It was the most humiliating turn of events for Djagad, to be struck by a woman first, and then knocked out again by her husband.

Idroes Moeria proclaimed to him, 'This is just so you know for sure ... I'm still alive!'

7

Independence and Proclamation

Everywhere, people were exulting with cries of freedom and independence. The most recent bit of news had roused everyone in M Town: Soekarno and Hatta had become the first President and Vice President of Indonesia, and Sjahrir was Prime Minister. The people hailed them as Bung Karno and Bung Hatta, calling them 'Bung', or 'older brother', out of admiration and affection for having declared Indonesia free. A new word emerged and grew quite popular: 'proclamator'. M Town was slowly getting back on its feet. The people began throwing themselves into their work once again, and this included Idroes Moeria and his wife Roemaisa.

Idroes had returned home still holding onto the dream he had envisioned two years previously, before he had been captured by the Japanese: the dream of creating real packaging for his klobot, a hard pack. This dream had only been reaffirmed in Koblen, when he had observed how the cigarettes available in Soerabaia had various kinds of packaging. A small Chinese boy had come every once in a while to pass him a fistful of clove cigarettes through the gaps in the wire fence. In prison, the cigarettes had been valuable to him. It wasn't just that they could be used as an improvised method of payment or as barter for necessary goods, but smoking a kretek could carry his thoughts home, to his pregnant wife, even if only for a few moments – although, of course, he did not know then that the baby had been miscarried, broken by grief.

One night, after making love to Roemaisa, he said to her, 'I'm going to change the name of our cigarettes. I do not want to call them Djojobojo anymore.'

'Why, Mas? That name is already well known in M Town. If you change it, we might have to start again from nothing.'

'Djojobojo is not a good brand name. I used to think it was good, but after I was in Koblen, I realized I was wrong.' Idroes Moeria didn't talk much about his days spent in Koblen. He preferred to focus on and enjoy the present – his wife, his house, his hometown of M Town, his klobot – as well as his future.

After all, he had not chosen the name Djojobojo at random. He had chosen it because he believed in the ancient prediction, that a bright future would follow the arrival of the 'older brother' who freed his people from the Whites. But before any such bright future had been delivered to them, he and his people had only been forced to endure more hardship than they had during the Dutch Occupation.

'So, what do want to call it, my dear?' Roemaisa asked.

Idroes thought for a moment. Then he smiled at his wife, clenched his fist and punched into the air. 'Independence!'

* * *

Idroes Moeria was busy making sketches on paper. He carefully drew the figure of a freedom fighter, from the waist up, with a red and white flag tied around his head, his hand carrying a bamboo spear. This would be the logo of the Independence! klobot he intended to sell; he asked Roemaisa to write 'Smoke

Independence! Clove Cigarettes' in her neatest handwriting below the picture.

The next day, he took the design to the printer. A child of about fourteen years waited on him.

'Where is your father, son?'

'My father hasn't come home yet, sir,' the child responded sadly. 'Did you ever see him when you were in Soerabaia?' Those who had their family members taken away by the Japanese often asked this question to the ones who had returned.

Idroes remembered he had been put into a truck with the other prisoners, and one of them had been the printer. But that was the first and last time he had seen the man for as long as he had been held captive. When he told this to the printer's son, the boy looked disappointed. He was only twelve when his father had been taken away.

'So, who is taking care of the printing now?'

'I am.'

Idroes Moeria smiled encouragingly, trying to give some motivation to the child, who had been tasked with a responsibility beyond his years.

Arriving home from the printer's, he wrote a letter to his friend in Soerabaia, a friend who had also lived through Koblen, and placed an order for 'papier'. These rolling papers would take the place of cornhusks in his cigarettes.

'What's this papier for? We make klobot cigarettes,' Roemaisa asked, confused.

Idroes enthusiastically informed his wife that the future of cigarettes was in kretek, clove cigarettes rolled in thin paper. Klobot cigarettes rolled in cornhusks were soon going to be a thing of the past. That was why he was asking for her to write 'Independence!

Kretek' on the packages, rather than 'Independence! Klobot'.

In addition to his enduring love for Roemaisa, there had been one more thing that had helped Idroes Moeria survive his time in Koblen: his plans to develop his cigarette production. He had turned his ideas over in his mind so many times, thinking about the things he would do to build his business if he ever got out of prison. In fact, he even felt *thankful* to have been captured and taken to Soerabaia – after all, if he hadn't, he would have stayed a simple villager who didn't understand the big city. And if he hadn't, even if he had achieved some success with Djojobojo cigarettes, he would have been successful merely in the tiny city of M Town, and would have stayed a big fish in a small pond.

During the course of his imprisonment, he had paid close attention to the habits of the smokers in Soerabaia and noticed that they rarely smoked the cornhusk-wrapped klobot anymore, and even more rarely the klembak menyan medicinal cigarettes. Instead, they preferred kretek, clove cigarettes rolled in paper. The basic ingredients were always the same: a mix of tobacco and cloves. Even their proportion remained the same: two parts tobacco to one part clove. It was the addition of a 'sauce', a secret combination of aromatic spices and other flavours mixed into the tobacco, which made a kretek unique.

Idroes Moeria decided that he would keep his kretek recipe exactly the same from batch to batch, unlike the klobot, which he had tended to mix with approximate measurements. Also, there were a number of different colours to choose from for the papier: black, red, green, white and orange. He decided that he would use red rolling-paper. He wanted to give his product a 'philosophy': to him, the slogan 'Smoke Independence! Cigarettes' and the red paper symbolized the struggle of the Indonesian people and all the blood they had spilled, here as well as in Soerabaia.

The following day, he went to the market to collect the Djojobojo klobot earnings. He once again ran into Soedjagad's man, who was also out collecting the profits from the sales of Djagad klobot and was re-supplying his distributors with new stock. But Idroes was shocked to see that his competitor's cigarettes had undergone a makeover too – now they had packaging, with classy writing that read 'Djagad Klobot Cigarettes' and an accompanying picture of Soedjagad's face.

But the concept of a pack like that had been *his* idea. He had come with it two years ago, although he never had the chance to follow through on it. He said nothing, but Idroes Moeria was enraged that Djagad had stolen his idea. Then, he looked at some of the other klobot being sold and saw that their packaging also displayed the picture of their owner. So it turned out that using one's own passport or identity-card photo was what everyone was doing now. Idroes immediately felt relieved that this hadn't been Soedjagad's original idea at all. The man was just imitating what was working for other people.

* * *

Idroes Moeria realized that M Town was very small, and not as progressive as the other cities, which had developed greatly over the years. In Soerabaia, people could become rich from selling cigarettes, and this was the case in Solo too. In Temanggung, people grew rich from selling tobacco to the cigarette companies. But in M Town, the brands of cigarettes sold in paper packs could still be counted on one's fingers. The people of this city, most of whom were farmers, still preferred smoking klobot to kretek. Some even still smoked kawung, cigarettes that they rolled themselves in palm leaves, buying the tobacco and the cloves separately. Sometimes they added rhubarb root and frankincense to enhance the taste of these smokes. But Idroes Moeria had big dreams. He intended to become a pioneer and innovate the clove industry in M Town. He was sure the other kretek businessmen in M Town would follow in his footsteps, but even so, he was sure he would not be defeated by them because *he* had the brains.

Roemaisa had grown quite anxious on seeing the new trends and fancy packaging of the cigarette trade. She blamed herself; during the entire time her husband was in Soerabaia, she focused all her energy on making sure the Djojobojo klobot business had survived. It hadn't occurred to her to create a nice package for their cigarettes. After all, she still had a necklace that could have been sold to fund this, even if her mother hadn't wanted to loan her any more money.

'Don't worry about that, Roem. We will surely beat the other companies and emerge most successful.' Idroes Moeria always said this to comfort her.

But how could Roemaisa not be anxious, especially when she saw the declining sales of Djojobojo cigarettes? In fact, their klobot had not really earned anything significant for their family yet. They weren't living off the sales yet, mostly because of the storm they had been forced to weather for the past two years.

'The packaging that you ordered has been ready for a number of days already, hasn't it? Let's start using it,' she urged.

'We will, but not until the thing I ordered from Soerabaia arrives. Be patient for just a little while longer, Roem. Can you do that for me?'

Finally the parcel arrived. It was filled with red rolling-papers and a few bottles of liquid.

'What's inside those bottles, Mas?' Roemaisa asked.

'This is the sauce,' Idroes Moeria replied with a smile.

The sauce? Roemaisa was intrigued. Then her husband disappeared into the storehouse, where they kept all their equipment for making the klobot. He only emerged from the room later that afternoon, and he brought out with him a few kretek. Yes, kretek cigarettes. Not klobot like before. He held two sets of four cigarettes in his hands, and he asked Roemaisa and his father-in-law to sample a kretek from each group.

'They are different, aren't they?' Roemaisa commented, after taking two drags.

'That's because of the sauce.' Idroes Moeria smiled.

'They taste like orange leaves,' Roemaisa declared in Javanese.

Then, his father-in-law chimed in, 'Wait, this one tastes like guava.'

'Really?' Roemaisa took an unlit cigarette from the bunch that her father said tasted like guava. The girl smoked it and agreed, 'Yes! He's right!'

The three of them unanimously agreed that the kretek with the flavour of guava was more delicious than the others. Later that night, Idroes Moeria made more guava-flavoured sauce so that it could be mixed into the newest tobacco-and-clove mixture the very next day. And so he had made Independence! clove cigarettes.

In a short space of time, the Independence! kretek became popular in M Town, and were soon selling faster than the other cigarettes in the market. And they didn't just have to compete with pre-made cigarettes; around that time, different kinds of rolling papers had been introduced, so people who wanted to smoke for cheap could buy their own paper from the market and use it, instead of cornhusks, to roll their own tingwe. Idroes Moeria discussed a partnership with someone from Magelang, so that Independence! cigarettes could be sold there as well. He was sure that if he could penetrate the Magelang market, it would be a great start for the further expansion of his business.

The brand name Idroes Moeria had given his cigarettes was perfect for the times. People were still heatedly discussing Indonesia's newfound freedom. The radio was still widely reporting on the recent occupation, the proclamation, and the possibility that the Dutch might return to Indonesia. The passion for nationalism was still a fresh fire blazing in people's hearts. Idroes had cleverly predicted this and named his business accordingly. Idroes was able to buy two necklaces, one for Roemaisa and one for his mother-in-law, who had loaned him the start-up money for his business long ago. Now, their small family could truly live off their kretek-business earnings.

Idroes soon had fifteen rollers working for him. Gradually, he earned enough to build a house out of sturdy cement bricks for his mother, in place of the old one made of bamboo and thatch. His father-in-law, the scribe – who no longer worked as one – said he would permit him to take Roemaisa to his mother's house once it was finished and was better furnished, so that she could live there comfortably. The scribe now helped Idroes Moeria with the accounting and had become his right-hand man of sorts. He was also one of the main investors in Independence! cigarettes. Idroes planned on moving the Independence! factory to his mother's house, where he would construct another building for the rollers to work in comfortably.

One morning, Roemaisa once again lost her appetite and

asked that the freshly cooked and steaming rice be taken away because its smell made her nauseous. The woman was with child again. Idroes Moeria showered his wife with kisses. The couple's hope blossomed again, and they wished for a child to replace the one they had lost three years ago. Their days were now bright and filled with cheer. Idroes could see his future – living in a nice house he had built with his own hard-earned money, with his loving family beside him. He now felt confident he would be able to comfortably support his aging mother and in-laws until the end of their lives.

It was true that M Town was only a small city, and it was easy for people to know each other there, but Idroes Moeria felt that he was becoming more well-known than he was before. That he was becoming as well-known as the scribe had been while working as a Dutch employee. People greeted him on the street, knew him as the owner of Independence! cigarettes, the red kretek – the red paper was attractive and popular, and that was probably why everyone remembered him.

One late morning, Idroes was overseeing the cigarette rollers and visitors to his factory, as well as monitoring the construction of his mother's house. As he stood in the doorway, smoking, two coolies appeared. They carried a large wooden beam for the foundation of the house, and one of the men asked the other if they could stop for a moment. They set the timber down, and the coolie took a pack of cigarettes out of his pocket, slid out a red cigarette and lit it. For a moment Idroes Moeria smiled, thinking that it was an Independence! cigarette the man was smoking. But then he glanced at the picture on the package and realized he was wrong – there was no bamboo spear on it. Idroes asked the coolie if he could look at the pack for a moment. There in his hand, it read 'Proclamation Cigarettes' and was accompanied by a striking picture of Bung Karno, the Proclamator himself, wearing his signature flat-topped, black peci hat, and with a red cigarette in his mouth. Then Idroes read the small print underneath the picture: 'Made by the Soedjagad Factory in M Town.'

In an instant he remembered the day he had punched Soedjagad in the market. He realized that his competitor, the man who had once been his friend, had returned the blow, and he had hit Idroes Moeria squarely in the face.

8

A Carton of Mendak Medicinal Cigarettes

Mak Iti', the midwife, arrived before the dawn call to prayer was sounded, and while the morning mist still blanketed the town. Three years ago, the old woman had removed the dead foetus from Roemaisa's womb. On that day, the latter hadn't shown any emotion. But on this occasion, she was screaming and yelling in pain, and it was her voice, rather than the adzan, that woke the people in the neighbourhood, making them leap out of their beds and get ready for prayer. This time, Mak Iti' had good news for Roemaisa's family: the baby had been born safely and was healthy and strong, even though the midwife said in Javanese, 'Oh, girl, your baby is wrapped in the umbilical cord. But it's alright ... It just means your child will look good in anything it wears.'

Mak Iti' cut the umbilical cord with a knife, and cleaned the baby's tiny body that was still covered in its mother's blood, then swaddled the infant in a batik sarong. The news of the birth travelled quickly from Idroes Moeria's house, as the baby's cries penetrated the mist, just as loud as its mother's screams moments earlier. Mak Iti' told Idroes Moeria to recite the adzan, the call to prayer, in the infant's ear. Then she handed him his child.

'Here is your baby girl.'

A girl. Idroes felt a stab of disappointment he didn't want to acknowledge, but the feeling quickly passed. Three years ago, when Roem was pregnant for the first time, Idroes Moeria hadn't especially wished for a boy. But after he had been imprisoned in Koblen for two years, he had hoped to have a son. Like many people at the time, he believed that a son would be stronger, more reliable, and would become the head of the family, growing into a tougher leader than a woman could ever be. But then Idroes remembered that he had lost his first child, and told himself he should give thanks for being blessed with another one.

Before she left, Mak Iti' said, 'I have put the child's placenta in a ceramic jar. Bury it in front of the house, and light a torch nearby so the air around it is bright and clear. Guard it from sunset till sunrise ... Do not leave it alone for a whole week.'

Idroes Moeria nodded in *understanding*. He paid her generously, and the old woman limped off alone, returning to her house. He asked a neighbourhood kid to go to the scribe's house and deliver the good news of his child's birth. His in-laws rushed over joyfully to greet their tiny red-faced granddaughter: her eyes were still shut, and her face still glistened, and her hair was soft and slick, and the skin on her scalp fragile. Every now and then, the little red mouth of the infant would pucker, and she would stick out the tip of her tongue: she was hungry. Roemaisa bared her chest so the baby could suckle from her ripe breasts. Her mother-in-law was overjoyed at becoming a grandmother, and in the early morning she went to the backyard to pluck star gooseberry leaves; she would brew them and make a tonic for her daughter-in-law to drink so her milk would flow better. She also had at her disposal a host of other health tonics: special jamu brews and elixirs for new mothers she had prepared weeks ago for Roem.

Soon, the cigarette workers began to arrive, and before beginning their rolling duties, they came to see the newborn. Mak Iti' came over every morning for forty days, to massage Roemaisa and help her body recover from the strains of labour. After she had been massaging the mother for a week, Mak Iti' also began to massage the infant. She brought along cooling powder, which came in little pellets the size and shape of goat droppings, and she mixed this with water then rubbed the paste all over the baby's body with her old, gentle hands, to make the little one feel comfortable and pampered.

Just as Mak Iti had instructed, Idroes Moeria stayed up all night to watch over his baby's placenta. Meanwhile, his wife, mother and mother-in-law took turns watching over the baby. According to tradition, in M Town, for the seven nights when the father was guarding his new-born's placenta, the other fathers from the neighbourhood would gather at his house and stay up all night long with him, giving him company. In return, the family of the baby was responsible for preparing all kinds of sweets and snacks and cigarettes for the guests. So, in the afternoons, Roemaisa's mother and mother-in-law, along with a few other women in the neighbourhood, would cook and prepare these dishes for their guests. As twilight fell, the men of the neighbourhood would arrive, and the women who had been asked to help would take turns preparing tea that was 'nasgitel' – panas-legi-kentel, or hot, syrupy and sweet. The men talked all night long, smoking, playing cards or checkers to pass the time.

Roemaisa didn't like this tradition. The noise made by the men bothered her; they were enjoying themselves and treating the house as if it were their own. She still needed a lot of rest after giving birth. Moreover, her newborn didn't yet know the difference between day and night, and was awake at all hours, making it difficult for Roemaisa to find a quiet moment to herself. And, of course, the newborn cried all the time – when she peed or pooped, and when she was hungry or tired. Only if everything necessary to make her comfortable was done, could the child finally sleep, and even then she would wake up one or two hours later. Unfortunately, the sounds of the neighbourhood men enjoying themselves at her house kept awake Roemaisa's little baby, and therefore Roemaisa herself. The smoke that was being exhaled by their loud mouths billowed throughout the entire house, seeping into the room where she was tending to her child, and making the baby cry on and on, possibly because she wasn't getting enough fresh air.

Roemaisa, who had always loved the smell of cloves, now wished they never existed.

When her little baby howled yet again after being startled by the men's loud laughter, she decided she had had enough. It was the final straw. The new mother burst into frustrated tears. Her mother-in-law understood why she was crying, picked up the baby and cuddled it in her embrace, singing to it softly. Roemaisa's sobs had just begun to subside when her mother entered the room and said, 'I am going home for a moment, Roem. I will bring back some sugar. We are out of it …' Then, seeing her daughter's wet eyes, she asked, 'What's wrong, my girl?'

Roemaisa shook her head slowly. 'I need to go to the bathroom,' she said in a barely audible voice. She knew she had to get control of her emotions. She wanted to wash her face and wet the crown of her head to cool herself down. She hobbled out, in part because she was still sore after giving birth and in part because she was trying not to let her sarong, which was tied more loosely around her body than usual, slip off her.

When Roemaisa stepped out of her room, she found the house full of the neighbourhood men. Despite the fact that it was her house they were lounging in, and that it was her family who was providing everything for them, they didn't pay her any mind. The place was so full of smoke that she couldn't breathe and found herself coughing uncontrollably. If she, who was a grown-up, was feeling so uncomfortable with the cigarette smoke, then she could only imagine how stifled her baby must feel, for the little one had just learned to breathe. She peered through the window and caught sight of her husband sitting outside, beside the spot where their baby's placenta was buried. None of the men was keeping him company. Idroes Moeria sat there all alone, smoking, and ever-faithfully guarding the placenta. Roem looked towards the men gathered in the front-room of her house and observed that not one of them seemed to care – no one even acknowledged her. It was as if they had come to do nothing but eat, drink and smoke at Idroes and Roemaisa's expense.

'Pak, could you please keep my husband company while he guards the placenta outside?' Roemaisa requested, speaking to one of the men. But he didn't even turn to look at her. He simply kept laughing and talking to the man beside him. 'Pak,' Roemaisa chided, but he still acted as if she weren't even there. Suddenly, she was furious. She could no longer hold back her emotions.

'Get out! Out! Everybody, out!' Roemaisa screamed at the top of her lungs. Now everyone was paying attention to her. In fact, they were gaping at her in amazement. Idroes Moeria hurried inside to find his wife yelling hysterically. 'This is my house! All of you get out!'

Idroes hastily wrapped his arms around his wife's body, to calm her. Then the woman collapsed. Blood flowed swiftly from under her sarong, pooling on the floor. Roemaisa lost consciousness. They carried her back to her room. After that, everyone dispersed, but most of them were leaving not to give Roemaisa a chance to rest but because they were annoyed by her outburst and thought she had been too harsh.

'She clearly doesn't know how lucky she is ... We were kind enough to agree to keep her husband company for seven nights,' one of the neighbours said on his way out. He continued in Javanese, 'If anything goes wrong, then they will regret treating us so terribly!'

The gathering was supposed to last a week, and Roemaisa had her flare-up on the second night. The following evening, she told her mother and mother-in-law that they needn't bother preparing food and cigarettes anymore, that they could close the door to their house. The women would take care of the baby in peace, without having to tolerate the clamorous voices of the men and their bothersome cigarette smoke, and without having to clean up the trash they had left behind in the morning.

Idroes was worried about Roem's demeanour. He requested her to be more easy-going, and to be patient with their neighbours until the seven nights were over. But Roem was stubborn. That night Idroes Moeria decided to visit one of the elders of the neighbourhood and ask forgiveness for his wife's coarse behaviour. But in order to do this, he was forced to leave his baby's placenta unguarded. And that very night, the thing they most feared came to pass. Idroes Moeria returned from the elder's house to complete darkness: the torch, which had been set neatly on the mound of earth covering the baby's placenta, was toppled over and put out.

And when he looked closer, he found that the mound had become a gaping hole – the dirt had been dug up, and his baby's placenta had been stolen.

* * *

M Town was in uproar. The placenta belonging to Roemaisa and Idroes Moeria's newborn was missing and now the couple, who had tried to guard it as best they could, desperately wanted to find it. Idroes ran around in an agitated frenzy, trying to look for who might have stolen it, while Roemaisa kept her eyes glued to her tiny baby, afraid that something awful might befall it. Unfortunately, the neighbouring men, who had been unceremoniously chased out of their house the night before, were only too happy to hear about the missing placenta.

'Look what happened? We were watching over the place but she sent us away. And now the placenta is gone!' They mocked and insulted Idroes and Roem in Javanese, and gloated like the winners of a competition.

As soon as she heard the news, Mak Iti' went straight to Roemaisa's house. She said she would guard the place until the seventh night was over. She asked for a glass of bitter tea and a pack of cigarettes, and Idroes Moeria served her this on a small tray. But when Mak Iti' noticed that the cloves he gave her were of his own Independence! brand, she refused them.

'Tomorrow, bring me these cigarettes called Mendak. The one with the picture of a dancer on the front of the pack. Bring them to me before the afternoon prayers.'

Idroes Moeria racked his brains. He was sure he had seen these cigarettes before. Yes, when he was a child, he had definitely seen someone light up one of those cloves, but he couldn't remember exactly when and where. He wasn't even sure whether the cigarettes were still being sold. He certainly would not have remembered them if Mak Iti' hadn't asked for them. He went to every single store in M Town, and every little stall and provisions shop, looking for Mendak cigarettes. He asked every peddler for them. However, most sellers were young and had never heard of them before, while the older ones asked, 'Are they still even being sold?' He was on the verge of giving up, but he didn't stop looking. If Mak Iti' said they were still for sale, Idroes was sure they must be, somewhere. That was what he told himself over and over, repeating it like it were a mantra. At dusk, as Maghreb was approaching, Idroes Moeria saw a shop at the end of a quiet road, on the outskirts of the market. The shop was dusty and quiet, as if left abandoned and forgotten. He knew from the looks of it that the store would sell betel, sirih leaf, frankincense and incense. When he arrived, a distinctive smell wafted out of the shop's door, a mixture of perfume and the pungent mouldy odours of the unkempt space. An old Chinese man was minding the shop. The smooth skin on his head and cheeks was dotted with brownish freckles, and only a few remaining wisps of long white hair poked out of his bald scalp. His eyes were practically closed, the puffy oily eyelids resting above two bloated cheeks. He was dressed in a sleeveless undershirt, which was worn so thin it was practically torn, and a shabby batik sarong that was ready to be repurposed as a kitchen rag. The man sat in a wicker chair in silence, a cane within his reach.

The light was beginning to fade as twilight fell.

'Do you sell Mendak cigarettes, Pak?' Idroes Moeria asked the old man, but was met with silence. After a few moments he was beginning to fear that perhaps the shopkeeper had died sitting in his chair. But then, to his relief, the man made to get up, with slow and shaky movements, leaning on the cane that looked to be about as old as he was. Idroes was worried it would break under the weight of the old man's body. His wicker chair let out a creak as he stood up. The seat was full of holes and looked ready to collapse, as if it had been worn down by the passing years and the unrelenting heat of a backside that never stopped sitting on it.

The old man turned, heading towards a cluttered corner of the shop. Idroes noticed that most of the things on the store's shelves had already expired and should be thrown away. The betel and sirih had started to shrivel and could no longer be sold, and some of the other items looked like they weren't really intended for sale anyway, but just piled up on the shelf for safekeeping. The shelves simply provided a perfect place for dust to settle.

For a moment, Idroes Moeria wondered if the old man had any family to help him take care of the store. He peered into the interior of the house, behind the store's filthy glass display case, but saw that it was quiet and there was nobody else there. It did seem like the old man was the one looking after the shop and knew where everything was.

When the old man turned back to face him, he was carrying a large carton of cigarettes in his trembling hands. He placed it on the counter and pushed it towards Idroes. Its plastic wrapping had a red label with the picture of a dancer on it, her knees bent, her arms extended, holding a scarf between her fingertips. The label read, 'Mendak Brand Klembak Menyan' and then in smaller writing, '100 Cigarettes'. A hundred cigarettes? That was too much, thought Idroes Moeria.

'Can I buy only some of it? I don't need so many.'

The old shopkeeper shook his head, refusing – although it was hard to be sure whether he was indeed shaking his head, because his head had been moving on its own accord ever since he had been awoken, and he looked very much like a baby learning to hold its neck straight. The man didn't speak, and so Idroes Moeria decided that he had in fact shaken his head. 'Alright, I'll take the whole pack.'

The old man turned around again, and with slow movements he took hold of a used calendar – the year printed on it was 1943; the calendar was three years old – and then ripped off a sheet to use as wrapping for the Mendak cigarettes. The old calendar was full of dust, and the Chinese man wiped it once with his bare hand, leaving one clean streak cutting through the dirt, then slowly began to fold it. Idroes wanted to rush inside the store and pack the cigarettes himself. He realized he was running out of time. Mak Iti' had asked for him to return home before the dusk prayers. But he let the old man finish his task.

'Just this. How much?'

With a stub of chalk, the man shakily scrawled a number on the surface of the wooden counter. That was what Idroes Moeria owed him for the cigarettes. The price was incredibly cheap. There were black liver spots sprinkled across the old dry skin of the man's arm. One of his fingernails, belonging to the middle finger of his right hand, was missing. Perhaps it had been broken off by a door or window slamming shut in the wind, the man too slow to move away, thought Idroes as he grabbed the pack of cigarettes and hurried off home.

Mak Iti' was waiting for him. 'Did you get them?' she asked.

He immediately handed over the cigarettes to her. Just then, the afternoon call to prayer filled the air. Mak Iti' instructed that for forty days, at every Maghreb, he and Roemaisa would have to watch over the baby together, and they must never leave her alone until the Isha, or the evening call to prayer, had resounded. She lit a Mendak cigarette and then placed it on the tray with the tea and other offerings. The aroma of the burning cloves quickly spread through the room. It smelled unrefined to Idroes Moeria's well-practiced nose. He could tell the difference between good and bad tobacco, and from the smell of these cigarettes, he could tell the tobacco used in them wasn't just bad but probably garbage, coming from a fallow field that should be used for nothing but grazing cattle. Or perhaps it had been taken from the leftover scraps of cloves from many different factories and then mixed together with the rhubarb root and frankincense.

At first Idroes thought Mak Iti' was going to smoke the cigarette, but she simply let it burn on its own. When the flame died out in the middle once, she quickly lit it again. Then, she used this cigarette to light another from the pack, and kept doing this through the night. In the early morning, after the dawn call to prayer had sounded, the midwife said she would go home and return later in the evening to perform the same ritual all over again.

Idroes Moeria and Roemaisa didn't really understand what it was Mak Iti' was doing. The woman hadn't even drunk the bitter tea she had asked for. She had been fasting all night as she watched over their house, sitting there in silence.

Only after the seventh night was over did Mak Iti' speak to Idroes: 'Your child's placenta was stolen by an enemy,' she said. 'This enemy intends to defeat you someday, and he will do so through this daughter of yours.'

9

Rolled By Hand

One year after the incident, Idroes Moeria still had three packs of Mendak Cigarettes left with him.

He and Roemaisa named their baby Dasiyah. He anxiously followed her development, worried that some kind of harm might befall his daughter. Every time the child seemed unwell, he immediately took her to Mak Iti,' if not to the local doctor. When babies fell sick or ran a slight fever, parents usually treated it with a familiar home remedy: they would make a paste of red onion, cucumber, fennel oil, coconut oil and white wood oil, and rub it onto the crown of the baby's head, so the fever would soon subside. But Idroes Moeria wasn't satisfied with such treatments. Instead, he insisted on giving his daughter expert care. The man had completely fallen in love with Dasiyah, guarding her as if she were the most precious treasure in the whole world, and one he was terrified to lose.

Idroes could not forget what Mak Iti' had said about his daughter's missing placenta, that it had been stolen by his enemy. But he never told Roemaisa about this because he didn't want her to worry. And yet, there was a name that haunted him, a face that followed him no matter where he went, and it belonged to Djagad of course. It seemed that the man would never leave him in peace, because just as Idroes Moeria was thinking about him one day, an official invitation arrived at their home, announcing the marriage of Djagad to a woman named Lilis. Unlike his small and simple wedding, it seemed as though Idroes's rival had invited the entire city for a grand affair. It was said his fiancé was from Madura, although no one knew how Djagad had met her. But everyone already knew that she was quite wealthy. Word was that she owned a scrap metal factory. To be clear, she wasn't the owner's daughter – she was the head of a factory in Madura herself. Roemaisa resisted when her husband suggested that they attend Djagad's wedding reception.

'But we can't *not* go. We have to show him that if he dares to invite us, then we will dare to accept his invitation. That we are not afraid of facing him!' Idroes claimed.

Roemaisa reluctantly went to change her clothes. A moment later, Idroes Moeria appeared at the bedroom door. 'Make yourself look really pretty!' he ordered. After he left, Roemaisa smiled to herself. She knew that her husband was still possessive of her and that made her happy.

Lilis was a voluptuous woman, plump and curvy. You could tell right away that after she became pregnant and gave birth to a child, she would get fat. She was the typical Madurese woman: a face shaped like a shield, with a frank and loud demeanour. Everyone whispered amongst themselves that she would be the voice of her family, which really meant that she would be the one to give the orders. It was also quite obvious to everyone that the woman was filthy rich.

Idroes Moeria ran into her a few weeks after the wedding, when he was collecting his profits at the market. He took a good look at Djagad's wife, giving her the once over. He had never seen any woman in M Town dress up in such vulgar fashion. The woman's lips were painted a garish shade of red, and her plump breasts looked ready to spill out of her too tight, too small blouse. She had rolled her sleeves up to her elbows, as if she were ready to strike someone at any moment. Her wrists were decorated with all the bracelets she owned – not just the bangles that were supposed to be worn in a bunch, but also gold chains that looked to weigh about four or five grams each. And she had not forgotten to decorate her neck either. She was wearing gold chains as necklaces too – five of them – with different pendants and charms. On the woman's fingers were lots of rings, all studded with jewels in different designs, so it wasn't clear which one was her wedding ring. The strange thing was, however, that although her ears were pierced, she wasn't wearing any earrings.

Idroes felt defeated. His Roemaisa didn't wear much jewellery nor did she look as rich as Djagad's wife. Before heading home from the market, he proceeded to buy his wife a gold necklace with a purple stone for its pendant. He brought it home and tenderly placed it around her neck. She blushed shyly at the unexpected gift.

'What is this for?'

'No reason, really. Does a husband need a reason to give his wife a little gift?' His answer made Roemaisa smile.

'Of course not.' But her question was answered that very night. Their lovemaking was impassioned, as if Roemaisa was giving her husband a special gift in return for the necklace. After they were finished, Idroes was lying on his back, gazing up at the ceiling through the mosquito netting, and Roemaisa was lying down beside her husband, pulling the blanket up so it covered her bare breasts.

'Djagad's wife is so tacky, wearing so many necklaces and

bracelets!' Idroes suddenly remarked.

Roemaisa smiled. She realized why her husband had suddenly decided to buy her a necklace. 'She's rich.'

'Sure, you can be rich, but that doesn't mean you go overboard flaunting your wealth. The thing is, I don't want you wearing as much jewellery as her. Just wear the necklace I gave you, and one bracelet. If you want to wear a different one tomorrow, go ahead. But just don't wear them all at once.'

Roemaisa kissed her husband's cheek. She knew from the way he was carrying on that he was jealous. She always thought it was adorable when her husband was overcome with envy.

Idroes looked at his wife in surprise. Her face still glistened with perspiration after their lovemaking. He began kissing her forehead, and then he pulled away the blanket that covered her naked breasts. He lifted up his wife's arm and inhaled the scent of her armpit. The smell of her body always aroused him. While his hands gently caressed her breasts, his fingers expertly played with her nipples. Roemaisa moaned in pleasure. And then began the night's second round of revenge against Djagad.

When it came to women, or more specifically Roemaisa, Idroes Moeria felt he had emerged victorious against his rival. He knew the kind of woman Djagad liked. Back when they were labourers and neither of them owned anything, the man had pointed out a number of different women he liked and, as far as Idroes Moeria could remember, they were all of a certain type: none of them was chubby or wore vulgar makeup, and some of them were even a little shy. So he suspected that Djagad had not married the Madurese woman out of love. Perhaps he had married her with another goal in mind. Of course, this was all merely Idroes Moeria's speculation, and it wasn't necessarily correct, but then it wasn't necessarily incorrect either. Either way, it grew out of his deepening feelings of jealousy and resentment towards his rival.

A few months later, Djagad sent out another invitation to the residents of M Town, calling them over for a mitoni ritual that would celebrate his wife in the seventh month of her pregnancy and would give prayers for the health and safety of both mother and baby. Idroes Moeria was once again invited, and he once again attended. He purposefully took along Roemaisa and adorable little Dasiyah to the celebration. He knew that Djagad was stealing glances at his wife, who was still slim and shapely in spite of having given birth to a child. Then, when she opened her blouse to nurse their daughter, Idroes caught his rival looking at her a few seconds longer than he should have. He immediately hurried over to Roemaisa and told her to cover her breasts with the batik cloth she was using as a baby sling.

When they were riding their bicycle home from Djagad's house, Idroes said to his wife, 'I think it's time that Dasiyah was weaned. She's almost two years old, and she doesn't need to nurse anymore.'

Roemaisa agreed. After that, she tried to make her milk taste bad: she no longer ate star gooseberry leaf; she stopped drinking her jamu tonic; and she smeared charcoal on her nipples, so Dasiyah would be repelled by the taste and no longer want to nurse.

Djagad's daughter was born, and they named her Purwanti. Soon after that, Lilis gave birth to their second child, and a third, and then a fourth and a fifth, all in a row. Right around the time when Lilis gave birth to her third child, Roemaisa once again found herself with child. She gave birth to another little girl. They named her Rukayah.

Independence! and Proclamation cigarettes had become the two main competing brands in M Town. Idroes Moeria had mulled it over, and decided it was time for him to further spread his reach and introduce Independence! cigarettes to other cities. It was true that Independence! was already being sold in Magelang and the surrounding areas. But Magelang was just a small neighbouring city, as small as M Town, and he couldn't sell many cigarettes there. Idroes had to admit that Independence! was still only a big fish in a small pond, even though the business had grown enough to comfortably support his family. However, he couldn't be satisfied with that alone. In the past, when he was just starting out and all he wanted was to win Roemaisa's heart by starting a business, perhaps that was all he had wanted. But not anymore.

He fixed a goal for himself: he wanted his cigarettes to be sold as far as Yogyakarta, and once he had achieved that, he wanted to further expand the business to Solo.

He began examining newspapers and magazines, studying the advertisements so he could use this knowledge to design his own. Idroes had decided to formally promote Independence! cigarettes to the public, and he dearly hoped they would be impressed enough by his advertisements to buy his brand.

Always Drink Independence! Cigarettes

If, Ladies and Gentlemen, you are tired after coming home from work, and want to feel refreshed, then you can freshen up by drinking Independence! cigarettes. Here's how: take one Independence! cigarette and light it with a match. Take a long drag, and let the smoke enter your mouth and flow through your body, then exhale slowly. After this, certainly, Ladies and

Gentlemen, you will find your thoughts have been refreshed. It is also beneficial for those suffering from asthma.

These were the words Idroes Moeria used in the advertisement he took out in one of Yogyakarta's local newspapers. Like other brands of the time, he asked people to *drink* Independence! cigarettes. The write-up was accompanied by a picture of the Independence! logo, of course. The ad would run every Sunday for five consecutive weeks. Idroes had his reasons for choosing the particular day. According to him, people would be more relaxed and in a better mood on their day off. They wouldn't be in a hurry, nor engrossed in getting their work done. Instead, they would have the time to sit in front of their houses and sip their coffee or tea, and perhaps even give their beloved doves a bath. Then, perhaps whistling to encourage the birds to sing along, they would leisurely open the newspaper they had bought from a paperboy.

He also started working with a supplier who could handle the sale of Independence! cigarettes in Yogyakarta. Before the ad appeared, he had ensured that his cigarettes were already circulating in the city. So if people grew curious about Independence! after reading the advertisement, they could buy the cigarettes immediately in their market or the closest shop. His cigarettes began to sell well in Yogyakarta, and he saw that the more well-known his cigarettes became in the big city, the more his sales in Magelang and M Town increased, growing by bounds. Idroes Moeria learned that this was the way the market worked; the people living in the rural areas followed the trends of the cities.

* * *

For the time being, Idroes was satisfied with his cigarette sales in Yogyakarta. Of course, he was not surprised to discover that Proclamation cigarettes had also started selling there. He tried to curb his irritation when, one Sunday morning, he opened the newspaper to find an advertisement for the rival band of cigarettes, complete with a picture of Bung Karno, the Proclamator himself, on the very same page that Independence! cigarettes were being advertised.

Make The Right Choice! Drink Proclamation Cigarettes!
The cigarette of Bung Karno and Bung Hatta.
Ladies and Gentlemen, without a doubt, you will know
what freedom tastes like when you drink
Proclamation cigarettes. You'd better believe it!

'Damn! This guy really likes to copy me, doesn't he?' he swore to his wife in Javanese. Roem knew that the anger was not directed at her, but at Soedjagad. 'Even after I knocked him out, he still hasn't had enough?' The newspaper he had been reading lay thrown on the table, a mute victim of the man's rage. Roem opened it up again and flipped through it until she saw the Proclamation advertisement. It was positioned right above her line of sight, while the Independence! advertisement was just below it. People who wanted to look at the Independence! ad would have to bend their heads or fold the newspaper.

'Well, it's already done, Mas, so just let it be. If you get angry, Djagad will feel happy, and if he's happy that means he has won, and if he wins that means ... you have lost.' But it was pointless for Roemaisa to try and calm her husband.

'I can't just forget about it! And how have I lost? Is that

what you think? I did not lose!' Her efforts had only incensed him further. 'From the very beginning, Roem! From the very beginning. Ever since I started making Djojobojo, don't you remember?' Roemaisa nodded. She wanted to say something but her husband kept on screaming, unleashing his ire. 'He has copied everything I have ever done. Right from the time I was writing on paper packs by hand to the time I started using nice packaging ... If I jumped into the Tegur River, I bet he would jump in right after me!' Roemaisa could not blame her husband for feeling angry. 'You mark my words, Roem, I will make another kretek, and it will *never* be beaten by that Djagad. I will make a kretek that he will never be able to copy, no matter how hard he tries!'

* * *

By the time Dasiyah was ten years old, she was already an expert at rolling cigarettes. She had been spending time with the rollers ever since she had learnt to walk. In fact, the worker women would watch over the adorable child as she took her tentative first steps, worried she would fall because she couldn't yet keep her balance. Now, Dasiyah had grown into a clever and agile girl, and so had Rukayah, her little sister. The pair often went to see the rollers and play with the cloves and tobacco. They would use the equipment too, and Dasiyah would begin to roll while Rukayah would trim, neatening the tobacco that was out of place. They would both ask for payment from their father based on how many cigarettes they had been able to make. Of course they didn't really work a full day; they only worked whenever they felt like it, but that was enough to make them both familiar with the smell and feel of tobacco, which stuck to their hands when they touched it. If on a particular day they were able to roll a fair amount of cigarettes, the palms of their hands would become sticky with a layer of clove and tobacco residue, which they would then scrape off with a fingernail or the edge of a spoon. Most of the rollers preferred to wash off the residue that stuck to their hands, but Dasiyah liked to let it accumulate. She had seen her father collect it from his hands whenever he joined in the rolling, and wanted to do as he did. And so it began, this practice that would turn Dasiyah into a cigarette girl.

When it was evening, and the rollers had all gone home, leaving the Independence! factory in silence, Roemaisa would prepare poci tea, brewed and served in a ceramic pot. For Idroes Moeria's taste, the usual one or two spoonfuls of tea leaves weren't enough, so she would fill half of the pot with them. Tea or coffee was indeed the best accompaniment for a kretek. But to know whether it was tea or coffee that was to be served, you had to look at the sun. If the sun was in the East, then coffee was sure to be perfect, paired with a clove. But if the sun was in the West, then tea would be the ideal choice.

Roemaisa and Idroes Moeria owned two tea sets for making and serving poci tea. The first set, a teapot and two small cups, was made from clay. The cups were so tiny that Dasiyah and Rukayah were often tempted to use them for playing house. But they both knew that when dusk had fallen, those two adorable ceramic cups had to be returned to the kitchen in pristine condition. The second tea set was Idroes Moeria's favourite. It bore a picture of three green circles on the body of the pot as well as on the little glasses that accompanied it. The tea set had been a gift from Three Ball Cigarettes, a company that had once been big and famous. In its heyday, it had given out many free gifts with its logo on them – small plates for snacks, lighter cases, tea sets like the one Idroes Moeria had. One could claim the gifts after buying a certain number of Three Ball packs – the biggest reward was a bicycle. Long after the company had to shut its doors, Idroes had saved that tea set as a fond memento of the brand.

Once Roemaisa had selected a tea set, she would fill half the teapot with tea leaves, then pour in boiling water to allow the leaves to steep. A pair of cups or glasses was then readied for the hot afternoon tea. The first glass was filled with small chunks of raw sugar, while the second stayed empty. Nasgitel – panas, legi, kentel, or hot, syrupy and sweet – was the most important rule of drinking tea. Roemaisa would pour the hot tea from the pot into the glass that was filled with sugar. After the sugar had slowly dissolved, she would pour this mixture into the second empty glass until it was almost half full. Then she would pour tea straight from the teapot into the second glass, mixing the sugary and plain teas for the perfect level of sweetness. To keep the water in the pot warm, Roemaisa would fold a cloth around the body and bottom of the pot. This cloth was never used for any other purpose but for the sole job of keeping the pot company.

To prepare the accompanying cigarette, Idroes Moeria would scrape the clove and tobacco residue from his hands, gather it on a piece of paper, fold the paper into a little bundle and then press the bundle under the hot teapot, placing it between the pot and the cloth. When the pot was lifted, the pile of clove and tobacco residue would be squashed down into the shape of a flat sheet, inside the paper, which he would then cut with scissors. He would mix these bits with some whole cloves and roll them into a cigarette by hand. After he had licked the paper's edge so his saliva would hold it together and keep the clove and tobacco residue inside, it would be ready: the residue would have turned into a delicious tingwe hand-rolled cigarette. And how could it not be delicious, since that tingwe was made from the true concentrated essence of cloves and tobacco, and not just from the regular tobacco-cloves-and-sauce combination like most kretek.

Dasiyah always paid close attention to her father's ritual. Then, one afternoon, she gathered the residue that was stuck to her palms and asked Rukayah to do the same. She gave this to her father, but Idroes Moeria hesitated before accepting it.

'Who does this belong to?' he asked.

'Rukayah and myself.'

'Really?'

Dasiyah nodded. 'But there's only a little bit. If you want, I could gather more from the hands of the other rollers.'

'No, don't do that!'

'Why not?'

'You can't be sure that other people's hands are clean. But if it is from your hands, or Rukayah's hands, of course I will accept it.' Dasiyah smiled on hearing her father's words.

That afternoon, she gathered more tobacco residue, putting it into the paper bundle, flattening it under the pot and cutting the residue that was pressed into a sheet. Then she copied the way her father rolled – she even licked the paper at the end so that the cigarette stuck together.

'Hmmm ... It should be really full, so that the cigarette looks a bit plump. This one is smaller than the ones for sale,' Dasiyah said to her father, showing him her handiwork. Even though this was the first time she had rolled the cigarette without using any equipment, she had made a neat job of it.

'You only need a little bit of the residue. If it's mixed with good tobacco that has our sauce on it, you can use it sparingly. It's actually more delicious if you enjoy just a little bit. If there's too much then it doesn't taste as good, and you waste it.'

Dasiyah nodded to show she understood. Idroes Moeria sipped his tea, and then he lit the cigarette his daughter had rolled. The smoke rose into the air.

'This tastes different.'

'Really?'

'Yes. Did you use a different kind of rolling paper?'

'I used the paper you use ... This one.' Dasiyah showed him the paper. 'Does it taste bad, Papa?'

'Oh, no! In fact, this one is sweeter than the others. I am amazed, my child.'

'Is it too sweet?'

'No, no. It's perfect. It's so much more delicious.' Dasiyah was delighted that she had been able to surprise and please her father. 'You licked and sealed this cigarette with your saliva, didn't you?'

'Yes, I did.'

'Ah, well, maybe it is your spit that has made it so delicious. It really is sweeter.'

* * *

Who knows whether what Idroes Moeria said was true or not. Perhaps he was simply expressing his fatherly love for his daughter, or perhaps Dasiyah's saliva really did taste sweet. What was certain, though, was that after rolling that first cigarette, the girl would join her father every afternoon for tea, and they would watch the day slowly fade into twilight. She wouldn't smoke, of course, but she would sip from her father's cup. Her little mouth would pucker and blow the steam that rose from the cup. Idroes was happy that his daughter was there to roll his cigarettes. Dasiyah also started rolling cigarettes at the factory more often, because she knew that the more she rolled, the more clove and tobacco residue she could collect. She would watch her hands, which would start out clean and then slowly turn brown, and then she would observe as the layer thickened on her palms.

One day, Dasiyah wanted to give her father a gift. It wasn't a special day. There was nothing to celebrate, and it certainly wasn't his birthday – like most people back then, Idroes Moeria didn't even know when his birthday was. If there was any date he marked on the calendar, it was market day. He didn't even know the exact year when he had been born. He watched the wrinkles appear on his face, noted if his skin was starting to sag, and counted the grey hairs that were sprouting on his head to approximate how old he was.

For one whole week, Dasiyah was truly industrious with her rolling. She even instructed Rukayah, who usually followed their mother around, to roll with her.

'But I just want to cut the tobacco.' Rukayah was already holding the scissors, ready to become Dasiyah's assistant.

'Maybe tomorrow you can do the cutting. Today you will roll, so that we can get a lot of residue for Papa, okay?' Eventually Rukayah agreed.

Roemaisa was amazed to see how hardworking her two daughters had become. She even had to remind them to eat lunch. And after they ate, they rolled some more. They didn't take any breaks, and when Dasiyah's schoolmates stopped by, the girl said she could not go with them to play. Rukayah, who seemed to be growing tired of rolling, looked imploringly at her older sister.

'Yes, alright, you can go. But first scrape the residue from your hands. Leave it here, please.' Dasiyah gave her a container. The younger sister quickly rubbed the sticky black layer from her hands, and then scampered off without washing up, heading to the stream to play and hunt for crawfish.

After a week, Dasiyah had collected what she considered to be enough residue. She asked the family servant for help, filling her father's pot with boiling water. And then, she scraped the clove-tobacco residue, which came off her hands like pieces of dry pasta, and then squeezed it under the warm pot until it was squashed into a sheet. After that, she cut the sheet into little pieces. Carefully, she began to roll the cigarettes by hand, making twenty little cylinders, shaping them as neat and nice as she could. Then, she put those cigarettes into a pack she had made herself, out of cardboard left over from a school craft project. Dasiyah even bought a box of matches to complete this very special gift for her father.

When the time came for Idroes Moeria's late afternoon rest, Dasiyah gave him his present. He was surprised and delighted.

'Rukayah helped me, Papa.' Dasiyah smiled, glad to see the exact expression of joy she had hoped for on her father's face.

Full of affection, Idroes picked up his daughter and sat her on his lap. He realized how much she cared for him. 'And what would you like in return, my girl?' he asked her tenderly in Javanese.

Dasiyah shook her head. She didn't want anything. She just wanted to see her father smoke the cigarettes that she had rolled and blow the playful smoke rings he would sometimes do to amuse her. Idroes Moeria did not immediately finish the hand-rolled kretek his daughter had made for him. He saved them for a few days, and every time he inhaled one of them, he savoured it in pure delight.

10

Kudus

It was a miracle that Tegar and Lebas had made it to Kudus without killing each other. Especially considering how annoyed Tegar became whenever his brother asked him to stop to buy cigarettes that had similar packaging to Djagad Raja's. Lebas had always wanted to sample the various kretek that imitated their brand, but had never had the opportunity to do so until now. During the journey he managed to buy a lot of cigarette brands in the small cities they passed through; these were local kretek that were not available in Jakarta but ruled the markets in their own hometowns.

He read the back of the latest pack he had bought. The brand was called 'Globe' and was the same colour as Djagad Raja, and even had a very similar logo – a globe, but without a hand carrying it. The background colour of the pack was the same as the one Djagad Raja used, and Lebas smiled when he saw this. He opened the pack, lit one of the cigarettes, inhaled and savoured its taste. It was obvious that Globe's owners had made a real effort to imitate Djagad Raja, but they had failed. The Globe cigarette was no match for the original flavour of a Djagad Raja.

'Mas, Mas, try this.' Lebas held out a cigarette to Tegar. 'These are Globe cigarettes. Damn ... they don't taste at all like Djagad Raja, do they?'

Tegar brushed his brother's hand away, totally uninterested. 'Don't bother me. I'm concentrating on the road!'

'Geez, fine ... Why do you always have to be like this,' Lebas muttered. Then he inhaled the Globe cigarette, pulling the smoke deeper into his lungs as if to swallow his annoyance at Tegar.

When the brothers arrived at the Djagad Raja factory in Kudus, two men opened a wooden gate covered in old, peeling paint to let them in. As soon as they entered the compound one hundred pairs of eyes, their owners' hands still busy rolling cigarettes, looked in their direction. A few of them were young women, girls really, who had just graduated high school. A few girls smiled at Lebas, blushing, and then whispered something to each other. Lebas returned their smiles. Tegar nudged his brother's arm with an expression of disapproval.

'What?'

'These village girls aren't here for your entertainment!'

'What do you mean "entertainment"?'

Tegar heaved an exasperated sigh and then walked away from the car. Lebas kept stealing glances at the young girls, and they kept returning the favour.

From inside the rolling room, an old plump woman dressed in a batik sarong and lace kebaya came shuffling towards them. An apron made of sackcloth was wrapped around her waist. It looked like it used to be white, but had turned a mottled brown from all the tobacco stains. A pair of thick glasses rested on her cheeks, grown thicker than the last time the brothers had met her. Mbok Marem spread her arms wide and greeted them warmly. A familiar aroma of cloves and tobacco enveloped the brothers as they returned her embrace. This was the aroma of history, Lebas thought to himself, inhaling.

'I didn't think you were going to come back here, child,' she said to Tegar in Javanese. 'I figured you liked it better in Jakarta.' She gazed at Tegar with tenderness, as if she were a grandmother who hadn't seen her grandchild in a very long time and was surprised that her little one was all grown up.

'Of course, I came back, Mbok. This is my village.'

Mbok Marem embraced Tegar affectionately again. She was indeed closer to him than to Lebas. He had practically grown up inside the factory, close to the rollers who had put down roots here. She was their oldest employee. Lebas had assumed she had already passed away or stopped working because of her age or health – and it wouldn't have been at all unusual if he hadn't been informed, considering how rarely he met his family. But it turned out that she was still alive, and still rolling faithfully for Djagad Raja cigarettes.

'Where's your father, child?'

'Father is sick, Mbok.'

'Oh dear, you don't say. What's wrong?'

'Health complications.'

'Is he in the hospital?'

'No, he wants to stay at home.'

'So if your father is sick, why are you here? You should be running the business from Jakarta.' Mbok Marem gave a sad little laugh.

'We are looking for someone.'

'Who?'

Tegar and Lebas glanced at each other, nervous. It was as if they were both thinking the same thing: if there was anyone who could tell them about the past, it was Mbok Marem.

'Her name is Jeng Yah. Have you ever heard of her?' Lebas

asked.

'Oh my!' Mbok Marem exclaimed. 'Never in my wildest dreams would I have thought I'd hear that name mentioned here.'

'What do you mean?'

'I thought it was forbidden to speak that name here. I thought everyone had forgotten all about her. You weren't even born when that whole Jeng Yah incident happened!' she blurted out in surprised Javanese.

Then the old woman started to talk. But first she made sure of something. 'Your mother isn't coming here, is she?' The brothers shook their heads, reassuring her over and over again that neither their mother nor father were coming to the factory. She also made them promise that they would never tell their parents she had told them about Jeng Yah. And then, Mbok Marem began, letting it all pour out like a leaky faucet.

'Jeng Yah is the owner of Lady cigarettes.'

'Lady cigarettes?' Tegar and Lebas looked at each other again, and then laughed at the odd sounding name. Many cigarette brands had strange, random names, and one could only guess what philosophy or history was behind them, and why they had seemed appropriate for the marketplace at the time. The name Djagad Raja certainly had its own long history and philosophy behind it.

'Lady cigarettes were once famous. Even I used to smoke them. They were around before Djagad Raja. They are not sold anymore, are they?' Mbok Marem wondered. 'But it's all right. These days there is Djagad Raja, and that is the exact same thing.' Then the old woman broke into laughter.

Lebas and Tegar wondered what she had meant by this. Perhaps, to her, all cloves tasted more or less the same, no matter what brand they belonged to, in spite of the fact that she had dedicated herself to the Djagad Raja factory for decades. But of course, if one asked Tegar, he would say with certainty that Djagad Raja Clove Cigarettes were indeed different, were more savoury and delicious than any other brand.

'Now, your father, well ... Mr Raja, it's believed, used to have a relationship with the owner of Lady cigarettes.'

'With Jeng Yah?'

'Shh! Don't say that name so loudly!' Mbok Marem looked around, as if she was afraid someone would overhear the gossip, even though whatever she was talking about happened decades ago, long before anyone at the factor was even born. Nobody knew about these things now except for Marem. 'They used to have a ... romantic relationship,' she continued in a whisper.

'See! I was right! Jeng Yah was our father's girlfriend,' Lebas said proudly. 'Mbok, do you know where Jeng Yah lives now?'

'I don't know.'

'Or, perhaps, where the Lady cigarette factory is located?' Tegar asked.

'Oh ... Well, it's certainly not in Kudus.'

'But our father told us that the last time he saw Jeng Yah, it was in Kudus,' Lebas said.

'As far as I know, the Lady cigarette factory is not in Kudus. It's in M Town.'

The brothers looked at each other in confusion. Then, Tegar remembered. 'M Town? Isn't that where our grandfather was born?' Lebas nodded in agreement, remembering too. But why would this Jeng Yah business take them all the way to their grandfather's birthplace?

'So we have to go there now?' he asked, meeting Tegar's eyes and immediately understanding the look they were exchanging.

'We have no choice, if we want to find Jeng Yah.'

Lebas knew his brother was right. They decided to stretch out and rest at the factory for a while. There was a house on the factory grounds kept ready for them to use whenever they came on a visit. The brothers had spent much of their childhood in Kudus, before Soeraja had decided to move to Jakarta in order to expand the Djagad Raja business. Back then, neither the house nor the cigarette factory had been as large as they were now. But as the Djagad Raja company had quickly grown, their father had bought all the surrounding houses and converted them into the sprawling property that stood there now, and the Djagad Raja factory had expanded rapidly. There was now a mess hall open to any labourers who had come for work from out of town. There was a clinic that offered free healthcare services. And on certain days, there was a pop-up market that sold everything from clothes to safety pins. There were countless food sellers who waited faithfully for the labourers to step out during their lunch breaks, ready to serve them tasty fare at affordable prices. The properties around the factory also housed small food stalls, offering impromptu meals, which always sold out. The regulars were all factory workers, of course, and the houses with sufficiently large front yards had opened parking lot businesses for motorcycles or bicycles, catering to those labourers who rode to work.

But they weren't all Djagad Raja workers. Their factory was one of many clove cigarette factory complexes in Kudus. Kretek, those little cylinders that measured no longer than five centimetres each, were the engine of the city's economy. And the workers weren't just from Kudus but came from faraway places like Demak or Rembang in northern central Java to make a living from cigarettes. In the mornings and afternoons, on the hot roads of Kudus, workers joked and chatted with one another, riding their step-through or onthel bicycles towards the factories. Some companies let their labourers wear whatever they wanted, but the larger and more established ones, like Djagad Raja, had their workers in uniform.

Not all the cigarette businesses were rich. Many of them had been around for a long time, but they didn't have the good fortune of Djagad Raja. Many of them struggled just to keep their factories alive, much less be able to produce television commercials; they didn't even have the resources to hire support staff. Some of the factories survived off their historical value, because many of them were founded by the previous generation, or the one before that – much like Djagad Raja, which was founded by the brothers' grandfather. But, irrespective of whether the individual companies were big or small, the clove-cigarette industry in Kudus as a whole employed more than one hundred thousand workers, thus providing income for almost two-thirds of the citizens in the Kudus regency.

* * *

Mira was one of the many pretty girls who was staring at and giggling at Lebas. They ended up chatting during her break. She was only eighteen years old. She hadn't gone to high school, and had only completed middle school. Lebas advised her to enrol in a program that would give her a high-school equivalency degree.

'It is a pity when a girl as pretty as you doesn't pursue her education. Certainly you don't want to be a cigarette roller for the rest of your life,' Lebas said. Then he called her Sweet Mira. The girl giggled at him, but informed him that she was waiting for her man to pick her up at the factory gate.

Tegar called his brother over with a disapproving gaze. Lebas found this odd, as his elder brother had always taught him to socialize with the workers and develop personal relationships with them. Perhaps he was cranky because it was Mira he was talking to. Lebas was forced to say goodbye to Mira, but just as he moved to leave, a Honda motorbike approached the gate. Mira hopped onto the back of the bike, sitting side-saddle, then smiled and waved to Lebas in parting. He nodded back at her and smiled.

'Don't mess around with these people!' Tegar said emphatically. 'I don't like you making trouble!'

Lebas snorted in dismissal, peeved that his brother was treating him like he was a little boy.

'How am I making trouble, Mas? I'm just talking to her.'

'The point is, I don't like it!'

'Whatever, weirdo.'

Tegar walked away, annoyed. He moved towards the factory office, while Lebas headed off in the opposite direction, equally annoyed.

11

Factory

Lebas decided to speak first and declare a truce between them. The brothers had been giving each other the silent treatment ever since their heated exchange that afternoon.

'Mas ... Come on, let's get some soto. There's no way we can come all the way here and not eat any Kudus-style chicken soup,' he said in a gentle voice.

'We should try some, shouldn't we?' Tegar replied. He sounded like a little kid, and it made Lebas want to laugh. He was pretending to be busy with the files piled up in front of him on the desk, making a show of signing them. When word got out that the CEO of Djagad Raja cigarettes had come over to the factory for a visit, the workers had arrived straight away, bringing with them all the files that needed to be signed so they wouldn't have to be sent to Jakarta.

Crack! Suddenly a rock came crashing through the window. Alarmed, the brothers hurried outside. They could just make out the silhouette of a figure on a motorcycle outside their factory, still wearing his helmet and poised as if ready to fight.

'Hey, who's there?' A security guard yelled from the gate. The figure remained silent. The other guard approached him, carrying his baton. Tegar and Lebas were beginning to feel worried and confused – what was going on? The figure seemed aggressive, intent on starting a fight with the guards rather than making to leave. Even from afar, Lebas could hear his name being mentioned. The brothers approached the gate.

'What's going on?' Tegar asked the guards. Now they could see the person on the motorcycle more clearly. He took off his helmet and approached Lebas, pointing at his face in anger.

'You better not think I'm scared of you! Just because you own a factory, you think you can steal my girl?' The youth accosted Lebas, speaking to him with a thick Javanese accent.

'Who's trying to steal your girl?' Lebas retorted brazenly.

'You think I didn't see you trying to get close to Mira, huh?'

So it was the same guy who had come to pick up Mira earlier in the day. Lebas hadn't recognized him at first.

'Mira is my fiancée, you get it?'

'Yes, Mas, yes! We can settle this peacefully. There's no need to get all riled up like this,' Tegar tried to intercede.

'If you come any closer, I'm calling the police!' One of the security guards threatened the man in rough Javanese, but that didn't seem to dissuade him one bit.

'I already told Mira she has to stop working at the factory, starting tomorrow! I can support her. She doesn't have to be a factory worker, making a salary that is worth little more than a piece of shit!'

Tegar exploded when he heard this insult. 'Hey! You think you're a real tough guy, don't you? How dare you speak to me like that? I pay all my workers fairly!' When it came to defending the factory, he was always up for a fight. 'Guards! Get rid of him!'

'Yes, sir!'

The security guards immediately shoved the man away from the factory gates. Grumbling, Tegar headed back into the house.

Lebas remained standing, still confused about how things had gone this far. He tried to apologize to the man; he knew that if he didn't, his problems with Tegar would drag on for a long time.

'Mas, honestly, I had no ill intentions towards Mira. We were just talking,' he tried to explain. He talked about how, as a co-owner of the factory, he was responsible for maintaining good relationships with his workers.

'Mira is mine! You get it?'

'Yes, Mas, I understand.'

'She is already tied to me. She owes me big time!'

Lebas gaped at him. What did the man mean by this? The guards pulled Lebas aside for a moment and explained in low voices, 'He's the local money lender in Kudus, Mas. He often loans money to the factory workers.' Lebas nodded, beginning to understand. It became clear to him that the folks opening up businesses around the factory weren't just cooks or people selling household goods but loan sharks as well.

'How much does Mira owe you?' he shouted to the man.

'Telung yuto setengah,' he replied in Javanese. Three and a half million rupiah.

'Wait here!' Lebas said. He rushed back into the office. He was in the middle of pulling out a leaf from one of the chequebooks in the drawer of the executive desk, when Tegar burst into the room. His older brother had probably come in looking for a place to calm down, but he soon became worked up again when he saw Lebas with the cheque.

'Hey! What do you think you are doing?'

'I'm taking care of a problem,' Lebas replied, moving swiftly. He knew he would have to be quick or Tegar would snatch the chequebook from him.

'What the hell do you mean? Lebas! Give it back!' Tegar tried to stop his brother, but Lebas pulled free. Just a few minutes ago Tegar had been trying to remain calm. Now he was being forced back into the fray. He followed Lebas as the latter strode towards the moneylender.

Lebas wrote out a cheque for five million rupiah and signed it. 'Here!' he said, handing it to the man. The young moneylender's anger immediately subsided, and his face showed amazement and disbelief. But after a few seconds, he turned tough again.

'If this cheque bounces, you'd better watch out!' Grabbing the cheque, he left, along with whatever was left of his anger. In the end he just seemed happy that his debt had been paid. Lebas then instructed the security guards to let Mira know about what had happened. Lebas was particular that they inform her she was free of the moneylender, so he wouldn't have emptied his pockets for nothing.

The security guards apologized for not being able to prevent the bothersome interruption. Lebas said it was all right, but asked them to be more alert the next time. Then, he walked back inside. He knew he still had some unfinished business to take care of – he still had to face Tegar.

'Have you gone insane? Using company money to pay off one of our employee's debts? Just because you are one of the heirs and have the right to issue a cheque doesn't mean you can do so whenever you feel like it! Do you understand?' Tegar shouted furiously.

Lebas rolled his eyes, tired of his brother's constant scolding. Since the beginning, he was the only owner of Djagad Raja cigarettes who hadn't been given cheques to sign or use, even though his signature was just as legally valid as his brothers'.

But in his heart, he knew that if he was permitted to have his own cheques, he would end up using them for other things, like making films.

'I already told you not to get mixed up with the people here! It's not that I forbid you from getting close to our employees, but this is exactly why I am always worried about you. To you, "getting close" means all sorts of things. If you could just act professional, then I wouldn't have to scold you all the time ...'

'I didn't do anything wrong, Mas! It was that guy who got hot-headed, because he is so possessive of his girlfriend,' Lebas said defensively. 'And what's more, the whole thing is already settled! I can even pay back our company money I used, if you'd like that. Just because I don't work for the factory doesn't mean I don't have any money.'

'This is not about money. It's about your behaviour! Who is Mira to you?'

Lebas pondered for a moment about what Tegar was saying. He had just felt sorry for the girl, that she was being forced into marrying some awful guy because she owed him money.

'When are you going to change?' Tegar went on. 'I thought the fact that you were willing to go look for Jeng Yah was a sign that you were starting to grow up. Clearly I was wrong!'

'Fine. What do you want to do now?' asked Lebas. He was starting to get angry as well.

'I don't want to travel with you anymore!'

'Fine, suit yourself!' Lebas stormed off, heading to his room. He wanted to throw himself onto the mattress, light a kretek and stay there, looking up at the ceiling, thinking bitter thoughts.

* * *

The next day, Tegar woke his brother in an incredibly rude way.

'How dare you spit on me?' Lebas fumed, wiping the moisture off his face and waking up with a jolt.

'What are you talking about? Spit? This is water,' Tegar held up a bottle.

'Knowing you, it's probably finger-bowl water that someone's already used to wash their hands ...'

'Okay, Mr Grumpy, it's time to get up. Sahur! Sahur!' Tegar enthusiastically sprayed his brother with more water, imitating the call during Ramadan to announce the pre-dawn morning meal.

'Alright, alright! I'm coming. But I'm still sleepy.'

'Look who's here.'

He focused his eyes, still blurry with sleep, and saw his other brother standing before him. 'Mas Karim! What are you doing here?'

'I missed you.' Karim grinned brightly. Apparently, he was very pleased with himself for surprising Lebas.

'That's bullshit!' he said. 'Why are you here? To make sure that Tegar and I don't murder each other?'

'Exactly,' Karim replied, laughing. Tegar's face turned grouchy. He had never been able to take a joke. He was probably still upset about everything that had happened the previous night.

'When did you arrive?' Lebas asked Karim.

'Just now. I flew in from Semarang and the driver picked me up and drove me here to Kudus.'

'What time is it?'

'It's already midday,' Tegar said, still cranky.

Lebas looked at his wristwatch; he had forgotten to take it off and set it on the bedside table. It was 11:22. It really was almost midday. Ah, he never could seem to get over his habit of sleeping late.

'Seriously, Mas, what are you doing here?'

'I want to accompany you both to M Town.'

'Why?'

'Well, Mas Tegar asked me to.' He gestured towards the oldest brother with his eyes.

'What for?' Lebas asked.

'So that everything is peaceful for a change. And so that if you are speaking nonsense to me, or if I try to explain something logical to you, there is someone to translate our words.'

Lebas laughed at Tegar's answer, but that only made him crankier. He realized that his eldest brother was not joking.

'So, when are we leaving?' Karim piped up.

'Tomorrow,' Tegar said firmly. 'At dawn. Now you ...' He pointed at Lebas. 'Even when someone wakes you, you still don't get up. So don't be surprised if I pour an entire tubful of water over your head tomorrow, instead of just dribbling a few drops from a bottle.'

Lebas immediately set his watch's alarm for four in the morning.

12

Lady Cigarettes

In total, Idroes Moeria had introduced six new cigarette lines after Independence! kretek, but none of them had sold well in the market. Instead, he only ended up wasting his money in his attempts to create a cigarette that would be undefeated by Soedjagad.

'Papa, why don't you just focus on managing Independence! cigarettes,' Dasiyah, who was now seventeen, advised her father one day. 'There is already a market for them. All you have to do is develop the brand further and introduce it to new markets.'

'But it's a new era now, Yah.'

'What do you mean, Papa?'

'When our cigarettes were first launched, our country's independence had just begun. Everyone was constantly shouting "Independence!" everywhere you went, so our cigarettes grew famous. But it isn't like that anymore. It's a new era,' Idroes Moeria explained.

'Well then, doesn't that mean that Independence! kretek has historical value?'

'I have to find a new cigarette that is right for today. Nobody talks about independence anymore.' He took out one of Dasiyah's hand-rolled cigarettes from a special container. Smoking his daughter's unique cigarettes had become a regular habit for him, and he rarely smoked anything else anymore. 'If you could make eight hundred of *these* cigarettes in a day, Yah, they would certainly become the number-one cigarette brand in Indonesia!'

Dasiyah smiled at her father's words. Since she had started hand-rolling her own cigarettes with clove and cigarette residue seven years ago, it had become a kind of special practice of hers. The father and daughter still carried out their afternoon teapot-ritual too. Only now she didn't just drink tea, but also joined Idroes in smoking cloves. However, she would not smoke the cigarettes she had made. Her father would not let her. So, Dasiyah only smoked Independence! kretek or one of the failed brands of cigarettes he had made.

Dasiyah had already tried her best to convince him that Independence! cigarettes could still successfully be expanded if her father would just focus on the one brand and not distract himself introducing new cigarette lines. She knew he wasn't even interested in developing a new sauce formula for these new lines; he basically just played around and did some guesswork, and mixed the sauce with a few minor changes, and then decided on the name of the new products: Rifle, Gramophone, Match head, Lucky 777 and Djakarta. It was a bit odd that Idroes Moeria had selected 'Djakarta' as a name for the latest line of cigarettes, despite the fact that the cloves were made in M Town. But people were now obsessed with visiting Jakarta, the nation's booming capital, so he thought that he could appeal to the clove smokers who had not yet had the chance to make the trip.

It was Dasiyah who would sample these new cigarettes, especially during the afternoons she spent drinking tea with her father. Through the process of doing so, her sense of taste and smell had become quite adept at distinguishing whether or not a cigarette was good. According to her – although, of course, she kept this to herself – none of the new cigarettes were better than the Independence! kretek, which she still preferred. She also knew that the hand-rolled tingwe she made herself were quite nice – how could they not be, they were filled with pure cloves and tobacco essence after all – but to her, they tasted just like the tingwe that her father rolled. So why did her father insist that the ones she rolled and sealed with her saliva were better? She wasn't sure. One day, she came up with her own theory: perhaps she was too familiar with the taste of her own spit, so she couldn't discern how it made the tingwe sweeter.

Idroes Moeria trusted his daughter completely. He had already shared with her the secret recipe of the sauce used for their Independence! cigarettes, as well as that of the other cigarettes that had failed to sell. When the time came to collect the profits from their sales, if he was feeling lazy, he would hand over the task to Dasiyah. Gradually, apart from simply handling the money she collected, she was also entrusted with the duties of allocating the money that was to be reinvested in the production of Independence! cigarettes, which was money that had to be set aside and not be used for anything else, and determining the portion of profits Dasiyah would allow her father to use in experimenting and developing his new cigarette lines. The girl had inherited her brains from her mother and her work ethics from her father, and because Idroes had trusted his daughter and given her freedom, she had grown into an independent young woman who wasn't afraid to have her own opinions. This was quite unique for a woman of that time.

'It's enough already, Papa. You can't make any more new cigarettes!' Dasiyah said to her father one day when he announced his intention to launch yet another line. After handling the books, she knew how to ration their financial resources. The cycles of experimentation and failure had taught her to be frugal. But Idroes Moeria had learnt no such lesson.

'This time I am sure it will be a success, Yah!'

'Papa, if you want to make another new cigarette, then you will have to take funds from Independence! And if this attempt fails, our production will suffer. And then what will we live on? How will we pay our workers?' She was resolute.

'So, what can I do?' He had never thought he would have a daughter with such a firm head on her shoulders. He was aware that Dasiyah was right, and admitted as much to himself, yet he insisted.

'Father, if you can find an investor, then go ahead. But you absolutely cannot touch a cent of Independence! money.'

And so that was just what Idroes Moeria did. He looked for an investor. He found a Javanese man named Pak Joko, who had married a Chinese diamond seller. When the man came over for a tour of their factory, Idroes greeted him warmly and graciously. He showed him around and introduced him to Dasiyah and Rukayah. He served the man tea, and took out a pack of Independence! cigarettes. He also opened a small box of Dasiyah's hand-rolled cigarettes and offered those to Pak Joko as well. This was the first time Idroes Moeria had ever offered his favourite tingwe to anyone else, but he wasn't surprised when Pak Joko was so impressed with his daughter's cigarettes that he refused to smoke Independence! anymore.

'Who made this tingwe?'

'My daughter, Dasiyah.'

'It's really delicious!' the guest said, examining the neat little cylinder in his hand.

'If you would like, please feel free to take the whole pack with you.' Idroes Moeria really knew to sweet-talk his potential investor. The man accepted the offer and agreed to take home with him the seven remaining tingwe that Dasiyah had made.

'I'll be back, and I'd like to bring along a colleague of mine, who really understands kretek. If he is in agreement as well, I intend to become your investor.'

Pak Joko left, and two days later he returned with a Chinese man who wasn't really his colleague but a family member – his wife's older brother. The man had no interest in trying the Independence! cigarettes Idroes Moeria offered him.

'I already know how these taste ... I've been smoking them for a long time. I want to try the tingwe that Joko brought home the other day.'

Once again, Idroes was forced to give up the cigarettes Dasiyah had rolled for him the previous day. He offered them three. The men eagerly lit the smokes, and then inhaled with pleasure.

'How many of these can you make in one day?'

'I am not the one who makes them. My daughter Dasiyah does,' Idroes replied. And then he called for her.

The girl appeared from behind the curtain, looking like a flower bud in bloom. Pak Joko and his brother-in-law were both immediately enchanted by her. Even Idroes Moeria was struck with wonder, for it was at that very moment he came to realize that his daughter had grown into a beautiful woman. It was as if he was seeing Roemaisa on the day he had gone over to the scribe's house to ask for her hand. He remembered how his wife-to-be had emerged from behind the curtain just like this, a flower peeking out from behind a leaf. The only difference between the two women was their expressions – unlike the shy Roemaisa, his daughter appeared with a bold and glowing smile, and was unafraid to meet the eye of her guests. Her face expressed wisdom – anyone could see that she was bright and clever. She captivated every man in the room in her own way, but elicited the same admiration from all.

'What is your name?' The Chinese man asked, mesmerized. He had already forgotten the name Idroes Moeria had just told them.

'Dasiyah.'

'Jeng Yah ...' This was the first time anyone had ever called her as 'Jeng', the term usually used to address young ladies. 'How many hand rolled cigarettes can you make in one day?'

'I could make a dozen at most,' Dasiyah replied without hesitation.

'Can you get other rollers to make them just as well?'

'Well, everyone knows how to roll tingwe,' Dasiyah replied. 'But they can't make ones this delicious!'

Idroes Moeria jumped in. 'First, these are filled with the tobacco and clove essence that is collected from the residue of a whole day's rolling. Second, if it isn't Yah herself rolling them, then they taste different.'

'You seal these with your own tongue, don't you?'

'Yes.' She gave a small nod.

'Why, you're just like the famous Roro Mendut! Idhumu legi,' he said in Javanese. Your spit is sweet. Dasiyah blushed at the comparison.

Everyone knew the story of Roro Mendut, the beautiful young girl from a small fishing village who dared refuse a powerful man. Centuries ago, Tumanggung Wiraguna, the great commander to the sultan, fell in love with Roro while passing through her town. He was rich and powerful but she refused his advances, declaring her love for a poor village youth named Pranacitra. In anger and retaliation, Wiraguna ordered Roro Mendut to pay a steep tax to the Mataram kingdom in return for her independence. Roro was a resourceful and clever woman, and she quickly hatched a plan. She decided to capitalize on her charisma – she would sell the cigarettes that she had partially smoked. Intoxicated by her beauty, men would pay a high price to smoke a cigarette Roro Mendut had already inhaled, hoping to have a taste of her sweet lips. However, she could only keep the commander at bay for so long, and ultimately she and Pranacitra ended their lives together, so they could always be together in death.

Pak Joko and his brother-in-law left after making some friendly conversation with Dasiyah. The girl was a knowledgeable discussant in all matters concerning clove cigarettes. If only those tingwe could be mass-produced, then surely the two men would invest in the company. But unfortunately that wasn't possible, and Idroes Moeria was left without an investor.

But he did not give up easily. He approached a number of other candidates, and in the same way, he lured them with Dasiyah's hand rolled tingwe. After a while, people began to come over to Idroes Moeria's wanting to buy his special tingwe and willing to pay a high price for a stick. He had never expected to sell these cigarettes for such a steep price, but people were willing to pay the price. They were intrigued by the reports of those who had already been lucky enough to try Dasiyah's tingwe, and were eager to taste these cigarettes for themselves. Every day there were at least five to seven people coming to their house, looking to buy the tingwe. Idroes Moeria had to disclose to them that the number of cigarettes his daughter rolled every day never increased, so he had to limit selling one smoke per day to each customer. Moreover, Idroes himself wanted to smoke the cigarettes his daughter made and no other kind of kretek.

Unexpectedly, Pak Joko and his brother-in-law returned to the house. Of course, the first thing they did was ask for the special tingwe. After they were done smoking it, they said they had decided to invest in Idroes Moeria's new cigarette line, as long as they could get a private supply of two tingwe a day each, and Idroes could guarantee he would repay the loan. Idroes Moeria was amazed that the men were willing to invest in a native Javanese such as himself, despite the fierce competition that existed between the Chinese business owners and the pribumi, or sons of the soil. He remembered how Pak Trisno, his old boss and the one who had first introduced him to the world of clove cigarettes, had told Idroes that in Kudus, in 1918, there had been unrest and even violence between the two factions of factory owners.

'I don't care if you are Javanese or Chinese, as long as I can make a profit,' Pak Joko said. Upon hearing this, Idroes Moeria felt the burden of expectation, especially because he knew that all his other cigarette experiments had failed. What would happen if this new venture failed too, and he was plunged into debt? 'If I were you, I would go to Gunung Kawi to pray for guidance before launching the new cigarette,' the Chinese man counselled.

At first, Idroes was reluctant. He was sceptical about making a pilgrimage to the renowned mountain in East Java to ask for good fortune, although he knew that many of the Chinese people in M Town went there. People would come from all over Indonesia to pray under a holy dewadaru tree at the graves of Prince Diponegoro and his advisor Mbah Djoego, to receive their guidance and blessings, particularly when starting a new business. If a leaf fell off the tree and drifted down to them, one knew their prayers would be answered.

But then Idroes Moeria decided that in order to show his investor how serious he was and to honour the trust he had shown him, he would set out to Gunung Kawi to perform the ritual. He took a bus from M Town to Yogyakarta, where it was easier to find a bus to Malang. From there he transferred to yet another bus and finally he arrived at Gunung Kawi.

It was the first time he had ever been to the mountain, and for a moment, Idroes felt like he had arrived in a foreign land. There was Chinese architecture all around him, and most of the people there were of Chinese descent. A few of the people there were advertising rooms for rent, hoping to earn a little extra from the pilgrims.

Before Idroes could see the grave, he had to climb a steep flight of stairs. Even though it was packed with people, the atmosphere on the mountain was pleasantly tranquil and quiet. Everyone was absorbed in his or her own prayers. The fasting and offerings had begun. Idroes Moeria was the only one who had come there carrying nothing. In all honesty, he didn't know what he was supposed to prepare or bring. He had purchased a plant from one of the locals hawking them at the roadside before starting the climb. Meanwhile, others were carrying everything they would need for their worship, including food that seemed better suited for a party, such as cones of yellow rice and whole roast chickens. The aroma of incense occasionally drifted past his nose. Idroes Moeria felt embarrassed that all he had brought was the one plant. Then he remembered that he had one more thing to give as offering: his cigarettes. Without hesitation, he took one of Dasiyah's tingwe and slid it in between the blooms of his plant. This was the best tingwe, a truly unique and special item, and so now he felt more at ease. He placed this offering next to the grave, alongside the ones already set there by other pilgrims.

He stayed in Gunung Kawi for three days, living almost like a beggar. At first he had wanted to rent a room from a local, but people said it would be better if he slept near the grave. According to them, this act would help convey to the gods that his heart's intention was pure. So he followed their recommendation, sleeping on the mountain and only briefly ducking into a local house to bathe. But then he started to feel foolish. He questioned himself about why he was sleeping rough, and whether it was even helping prove his genuine participation in the pilgrimage. Eventually, Idroes Moeria decided to obtain better accommodation. He rented himself a room where he could sleep comfortably and bathe whenever he needed to, and – since the people renting out the rooms also provided food – could eat a proper meal.

He now felt more devout and focused when he prayed. On the seventh night, the night before Idroes Moeria was to return home to M Town, he decided that even if he ended up returning home empty-handed, that would be all right. He had to accept everything that happened to him with equanimity, even if that meant he would have to make another pilgrimage to receive a sign or a blessing. He submitted himself to fate. But later that evening, after he had made that reconciliation, he was visited by his daughter Dasiyah in a dream. She had grown into a beautiful young woman. She lit a kretek that she had rolled herself, inhaled deeply, and then blew the smoke over Idroes Moeria's face. This jolted him awake, and he thought he could still smell the aroma of cloves and even see the smoke, but it turned out that what was around him was only a thin layer of cold morning fog that had crept into his room.

That morning, before Idroes Moeria headed home to M Town, he once again visited the grave of Grandfather Djoego. As he took his leave, he said goodbye to one of the caretakers who was diligently sweeping near the grave and gave him all the money he had. He also recounted how he had dreamt of his daughter.

'Maybe it's because I miss her so much,' he said. He could still remember the aroma of Dasiyah's sweet tingwe. He hadn't tasted the cigarettes since he ran out of them four days ago.

'Or maybe, sir, you should name your new venture after your daughter ...'

Idroes was flabbergasted. Really? Was this what the dream had meant? 'Have I been blessed with a sign?' he asked. 'But not even a single leaf of the dewadaru tree fell down to me.'

'Well, a blessing can come in any form. Even in a dream.'

* * *

When he arrived home, Idroes Moeria began to brainstorm names that were related to his daughter. Of all the names he was considering, Dasiyah Cigarettes seemed like the strongest contender by far.

'How about it? Do you like the name? It's good, isn't it? Your name would be on the label, and we could use your photograph as the image on the pack, if you'd like.'

'Oh, Papa, that's so old-fashioned! How would that be any different from Djagad Cigarettes?' Idroes Moeria became deflated, remembering his competitor's packaging with Soedjagad's likeness on the label. His daughter was right. That would be a step backwards for their brand. Things had moved on. 'Plus, I'm a lady now, Father. I'd be embarrassed if my face was stuck on the label.'

'A lady?'

'Yes ...' Dasiyah bowed like a hibiscus flower, suddenly shy.

'You indeed are a lady now. But you'll always be my little cigarette girl,' Idroes said. 'Wait, I've got it! We'll call them Lady cigarettes.' Dasiyah approved of the name, but only as long as her face wasn't used on the label.

Idroes Moeria agreed to her condition. Instead he drew a young woman who bore a striking resemblance to his daughter. She was wearing a lace kebaya blouse, and her hair was pulled back in a small but neat chignon, and she was holding a lit cigarette with a wisp of smoke rising from its tip.

Dasiyah's second stipulation was that she wanted to be involved in the making of the sauce. According to her, the sauces used in the different experimental cigarettes had been of inferior quality and taste.

'So, of course, those cigarettes were destined to fail,' she said. She added that from then on her father wouldn't just half-heartedly make new cigarettes whenever he wanted and then sell them just to watch them fail. This time someone else's money was involved, a loaned investment, and he could not risk failing. Hearing her reasoning, Idroes Moeria's realized that his daughter had blossomed into a mature and thoughtful woman before his very eyes.

'Well, what do you want to do about the sauce then?'

It turned out that Dasiyah had been secretly mixing different kinds of ingredients, trying to create her own sauce. She had taken the Independence! sauce as the base and then added to it other elements to enhance the taste. She had tried to determine what it was about her tingwe that the investor liked so much: it was sweeter than other cigarettes but also more savoury and aromatic, and the clove and tobacco essence surely contributed to its superior flavour. She had tried to use a new combination of ingredients to recreate the taste of her special cigarettes.

Her father tried one and said, 'While this isn't exactly like your hand-rolled cigarettes, it's still quite tasty. Where did you learn to blend sauce so well?'

'From all the mistakes that you made, Papa.'

They both agreed that Dasiyah had created the sauce they would use in their new Lady cigarettes.

Idroes Moeria's dream of making a clove cigarette that could never be beaten by Soedjagad was soon to be realized. The investor gave them a little extra money to advertise:

Lady Cigarettes
Inhale just once
and the lady of your dreams
will appear before you.

In the past, the cigarette companies had used the word 'drink' to refer to their products, which of course had nothing at all to do with liquid. However, now there was a more appropriate word that was coming into use: 'inhale'. Moreover, their new advertisement wasn't like most others, which were usually verbose, using a lot of words to describe their product. This advertisement only had one sentence, along with the picture of a Lady cigarettes pack. It was successful at luring in new customers, who flocked in droves to buy the brand, even though, after smoking multiple packs, the girl of their dreams never really appeared before them.

Dasiyah regularly purchased copies of the magazines that featured their advertisements. But one day, while flipping through the pages of a magazine to find the Lady cigarettes advert, her eyes fell upon an advertisement for another new brand of cigarettes:

Garwo Kulo Cigarettes
The cigarette for the man who loves his wife.

Garwo kulo meant 'my woman' or 'my wife' in Javanese. Across the bottom of the advertisement, written in small print, was 'Made by Djagad Cigarettes, M Town.' There was also a drawing of a woman – it wasn't exactly a portrait but more like a faded photograph that had been sketched over to make the facial features more prominent. It was the face of Soedjagad's wife, the hefty and garish woman from Madura.

Dasiyah quickly informed her father of what she had found. Idroes hurled the magazine to the floor in anger. 'Once again he copies me! Again and again!'

Her father's rage was certainly justified. With a name like that, it was clear that Soedjagad intended to capture the Lady cigarette market. But this time Idroes Moeria did not have to worry, because Garwo Kulo failed to sell. This time, Djagad had misread his consumers. When men smoked, they wanted their thoughts to move freely, to float in the air with the rising smoke. When they saw the ad for Lady cigarettes, people were inspired to fantasize about a stylish, young, beautiful woman, someone who aroused them and made them feel masculine. On the other hand, when they saw Garwo Kulo, or My Woman, they were reminded of their wife at home, who rarely wore makeup, dressed slovenly and never stopped nagging them.

The sales of Lady cigarettes skyrocketed, and Dasiyah grew busier and busier promoting the cigarettes at the occasional night markets that came to town – not just in M Town, but also in Yogyakarta, Magelang, Solo, Kudus and as far away as Lampung. Letters from Banyuwangi and Kalimantan poured in, reporting that Lady cigarettes were selling well there too and asking for the rights to become city distributors.

Rukayah, who was now entering adolescence, got her father's permission to join Dasiyah at the night fairs. The girl was old enough to attract new customers. Then Dasiyah had an idea: rather than employing men to promote Lady cigarettes, she would hire Rukayah's friends. This would fit the brand's image. On observing this strategy, some of the other cigarette companies that had stands in the night market also switched to hiring young ladies to promote their cigarettes.

Because M Town was a small city, the fair was held there once a year at most, usually around August 17, Indonesian Independence day. When the time came, Dasiyah ensured that Lady cigarettes were available for sale. She became quite popular amongst the other stallholders. Everyone knew that if there was one woman who ran a professional cigarette stand it was Jeng Yah, which was what everyone called her now.

On the second day of the fair in M Town, around dinnertime, a young man showed up wearing shabby clothes and carrying a bundle over his shoulder. With the money he could scrape from his pockets, he bought some pecel, or rice with tofu and vegetables flavoured with spicy peanut sauce and wrapped in a banana leaf. Then, with the money he had left over, he approached the Lady cigarettes stand. He had noticed the pretty women working there, and it was only natural that a young man his age would be interested in meeting them.

'Would you like a Lady cigarette, Mas?' Jeng Yah greeted him in a friendly, melodious voice.

The youth searched the pockets of his shabby jacket and found nothing but one silver coin. Of course, he didn't have enough to buy a pack, and at the night market nobody sold loose cigarettes, so he couldn't ask to buy just one.

'Or perhaps you'd like to play the ring toss?' Jeng Yah offered. Even though it was really just a marketing ploy, the youth still felt like it was a challenge, and Jeng Yah flashed him a coy smile as if to say as much. He gave her his silver coin and received five rings to toss towards the targets that were lined up before him. If he won, he wouldn't just receive a pack of cigarettes, but also different bottled drinks, cotton candy and perhaps even a toy.

The first toss. He missed. Jeng Yah smiled.

The second toss. He missed, and then looked over at Jeng Yah. 'Try again, there are still three rings left,' she said. She meant to encourage him, but he felt like the pretty girl was mocking him.

He threw the third, the fourth, and the fifth rings. He missed again.

'Aah …' he cried, disappointed.

'Oh well, thank you for playing.'

The youth made to leave. But then Jeng Yah called to him, 'Just a moment.'

'What is it?'

'Here.' Jeng Yah held out a pack of Lady cigarettes.

'You don't have to do this.'

'It's nothing. Just take it. Think of it like you won the ring toss.'

The young man shook his head. 'Your boss will be angry with you.'

'I am the boss here. So no one will be angry with me.'

The youth was impressed. 'This is your stand?'

'Yes.' He accepted the cigarettes and left.

In the days that followed, Jeng Yah saw him hanging around the stalls. Sometimes he would be hauling sacks for stand owners. Other times, as the day turned to dusk, he could be found helping them set up a stand and then, as morning approached, he would be there breaking it down again.

Jeng Yah noticed how every time the youth met her gaze, he gave a small nod, a show of respect. He was clearly diligent and polite, she thought. Then one afternoon, he was free to help Jeng Yah set up her stand, and that was when she got the opportunity to speak with him again.

'What's your name?'

'Raja,' he said. 'My full name is Soeraja, and is pronounced as "Suraya".'

'I'm ...'

'Jeng Yah. Am I right?' Raja said quickly. The girl blushed and nodded. Typical of someone with a crush, the man had done his homework. He had learned whatever he could about the girl he liked.

After that, Soeraja always waited for Jeng Yah to arrive, in order to help her open her cigarette stand. If anyone else arrived first and asked for his services, he would always come up with an excuse so that when Jeng Yah showed up, he would be free. A week later, everyone knew that Raja only worked for Lady cigarettes. Without Raja asking for it, Jeng Yah also gave him a small amount as payment.

By the end of August, the red and the white flag was taken down and folded up neatly. The night market was coming to a close. The games and entertainment stalls were dismantled and packed away, to be stored in boxes and saved for the next season. The stand owners were winding up, preparing to move on to the next small city-square. To Raja, who had been living at the fair for a month now, it suddenly felt like his house was being torn apart before his very eyes. The town square soon lay bare and deserted.

'Where will you go now?' asked Jeng Yah.

'I don't know yet.' He wanted to say that he didn't want to leave M Town at all, and that he had already found for himself there a house without a roof, a home for his heart, and that after the night market dispersed, and Roemaisa had left him, he would feel very lonesome indeed. But he said none of this to her.

Then, she asked him, 'Would you like to come work for me?'

Jeng Yah watched Raja's smile spread across his face, but she didn't quite realize that the young man's heart was overflowing with great delight.

14

Dasiyah and Soeraja

Everyone knew Dasiyah, the flower of M Town, the beautiful daughter of the popular clove cigarette businessman. She was a cheerful girl, friendly to whomever she met. Her smile never vanished from her lovely face. It stayed in place like an embellishment, much like a necklace or a pair of earrings.

Idroes Moeria no longer worried that his wife hadn't given birth to any sons. It was enough for him that he had Dasiyah. The girl was not a tomboy at all, but she had the energy of a first-born son and could take care of their family. He could see that his daughter possessed wisdom and good instinct, which was valuable in managing their family cigarette-business.

When the night fair in M Town was over, and there was no place left for Soeraja to stay, Dasiyah decided to offer him work and shelter.

'Are you sure you want him to live here?' asked Idroes Moeria when his daughter told him about Soeraja's sorry state and that the youth was all alone in world. 'You realize, don't you, that this would mean taking in a stranger? If he turns out to be a bad man, what then?' He glanced over at Soeraja, who looked as if he were waiting for a judge's verdict.

'He's a hard worker, Papa. At the night market, I observed that he never stopped helping people. I feel bad that he doesn't have a place to stay. He can sleep in the storehouse and help out with whatever we need. I'm sure he will make himself useful.'

Idroes was genuinely concerned. As a father of two young women in the flower of their youth, he didn't want an unfamiliar young man to suddenly make his way into their household, and live and eat and sleep amongst them. He didn't want any uncharitable gossip about his daughters making its way around town, especially now that the Lady cigarette business was booming.

Soeraja finally spoke up for himself. 'I can sleep in the mosque down the road, sir. I don't have to live here in your house. But please, give me some work. I'll do whatever you want me to.'

And so Idroes Moeria agreed. Soeraja could work for them, but he couldn't live with them. Dasiyah smiled at the young man as her father made his final decision. She was pleased that the wandering youth had decided to stay put and work for her, and that he would be by her side every day. Secretly, she had already fallen in love with him.

Once he started working for their family, Dasiyah always made herself available to chat with Soeraja. She loved listening to the tales of his journeys. He had gone from one city to another, leaving behind the place where he was born. His entire life was packed up in one small bundle; it was if that bundle was the small world that he carried with him wherever he went, a world that could be disassembled and reassembled at every place he stopped. She realized that there was a part of her that wanted the life Soeraja had lived: roaming and wandering, free and independent.

One day, Dasiyah was rolling the special clove cigarettes filled with the kretek residue that she always made for her father. But this time something had changed – she wasn't making this batch of tingwe for Idroes Moeria, but for Soeraja. When they were ready, she handed it to him. The man struck a match, lit her cigarette and smoked it.

'I am completely certain that Roro Mendut has been reincarnated in you, Jeng.'

'What do you mean?'

'This is the sweetest and most delicious tingwe I have ever tasted.'

'The sauce I used in it is the same one we use for Lady cigarettes.'

'It's not that ... There is something else about this tingwe that is special. You licked the paper to hold it together, right?'

'Yes.'

'See, that is why I am so sure that you are the reincarnation of Roro Mendut, the beautiful lady who lived for cigarettes and has sweet spit.' Dasiyah blushed. 'I am sure that if you went to the market and sold your half-smoked cigarettes like Roro Mendut did, you would get a lot of money for them.'

She smiled. She knew that she was being flattered. 'I would never sell my cigarette butts like Roro Mendut.'

'Well, of course not, but you are still just like her... Jeng Yah and Roro Mendut. What makes both your cigarettes taste so good is your incredibly sweet saliva.'

'Men just imagine that because they know the tingwe has touched a woman's lips,' Dasiyah demurred. Soeraja laughed. He glanced down at the tingwe clove that rested between his fingers.

'Do you know the history of cloves?' he asked. Dasiyah shook her head.

Soeraja took a pleasurable drag on his cigarette. Dasiyah struggled to contain her delight when she saw how much the young man enjoyed the cigarette she had rolled for him. All this time, even as people had been lining up to order her tingwe, she had never felt so overwhelmed with joy as she did now.

'Long ago, in Kudus, there was a certain Mr Haji Jamari,' Soeraja began. 'He lived in the late eighteen hundreds ...' Dasiyah listened to Soeraja spin his fairytale about clove cigarettes. About how Jamari had difficulty breathing, and was looking for a way to get woor, or cloves, which are known for their soothing properties into his lungs. He had chopped up some and mixed them with tobacco and then rolled it all up in a cornhusk. When the flame ignited this hand-rolled cigarette, he had heard a soft crackling sound, kretek-kretek, from the burning slivers of clove inside. That was the beginning of kretek.

Dasiyah knew everything there was to know about kretek: their aroma, taste, their texture in her hand, their texture on her lips, the smoothness of their smoke, the physical sensation when the smoke came out of her mouth and her nose, the inner sensation that came with the smoking, the feeling of peace that accompanied the very first drag. But she had never really known the origins of kretek. It was only from this wanderer that she had learnt the story. Who knew whether it was true or not, but she wanted to believe it.

'How do you know this?' she asked.

'I've been to Kudus. Where Pak Jamari is from.'

Dasiyah looked surprised and interested. 'Did you meet his family?'

'No. I just met people who knew Pak Jamari. Most of them were already quite old.'

'Is Pak Jamari still alive?' Dasiyah asked.

'I don't know. If he is, then he must be ancient.'

'I want to meet him, if he's still alive.'

'If he's still alive, I will take you.'

Dasiyah smiled, and then that smile turned into a hot blush she could not hide. Now the girl knew that the young man liked her too.

* * *

Idroes Moeria counted the tingwe that Dasiyah had made. Usually, Dasiyah brought him seven to nine of his beloved cigarettes, but this time there were only six. Something was wrong, and Idroes was suspicious.

'Maybe this is all she was able to make today,' said Roemaisa. 'You don't always get a lot of residue.'

'No. I am sure Yah must have made more than six. I think she has given the rest to someone else.'

Roemaisa shook her head, trying to understand her husband. 'Who?'

'Someone.'

'Who?'

'How should I know?' Idroes snapped.

Actually, he did have an inkling, but he was trying to deny it: she must have given those tingwe to Soeraja. He hadn't liked the boy from the very first moment he had met him. Dasiyah had fallen for him too quickly.

Idroes Moeria's suspicions were not wrong, because at that very moment Dasiyah was sitting with Soeraja, blushing. She had stared setting aside a few cigarettes for Soeraja for a while now. At first it had just been one, and then two, and then three. Her reason was simple: he really enjoyed the cigarettes she rolled.

But then, who didn't? Everyone did. It had been those tingwe, after all, that had gotten Idroes Moeria the start-up money for Lady cigarettes.

'I'm lucky that I have come to know Roro Mendut so well.'

'What do you mean? Roro Mendut?'

'I mean you, silly ... My cigarette girl!' Soeraja said, and then took a long drag off the special tingwe that Dasiyah had brought for him.

She blushed on hearing him say 'my cigarette girl'. Lately, it seemed like she was blushing all the time, even when she wasn't with Soeraja. She would replay their past meetings in her mind, and suddenly would remember something that Raja had done to make her blush the day before, or the week before, or earlier that morning, and then she would find herself blushing again, and because it was happening in her mind she felt like she was allowed to blush for as long as she wanted, especially since there was no one there to see her. Her little sister Rukayah was the only one who often came across Dasiyah blushing alone. But then the latter would say that Rukayah was too young to understand why.

In Soeraja, she had found her own private storyteller, one who knew a thousand and one tales, and all just for her. The girl was intoxicated with the way he told his stories. Whatever it was he was talking about became all the more interesting when he was narrating it. If she told Rukayah one of the stories Raja had told her, her sister would simply lift her chin and wrinkle her forehead, and ask, 'What is so good about this story?'

'You silly kid!' Dasiyah would reply in annoyance, and then she would leave her ignorant sister still mulling over the tale.

* * *

Idroes Moeria could no longer hold back his curiosity about Dasiyah and Soeraja. So one afternoon, when he saw his daughter chatting intimately with the boy, he beckoned the two young people to come over and speak with him. They both put on their most innocent expressions, but Idroes wasted no time with small talk and asked bluntly: 'Are you two sweethearts?'

For a few seconds they laughed nervously, just looking at each other and at Idroes Moeria, who just stood there, impassive and ramrod straight like a cigarette. Then their laughter stopped, and then Dasiyah's throat let out a sudden gasp. She was still looking at Soeraja, and both their cheeks were blushing red from embarrassment. The problem was that they had never discussed with one another whether they were a couple. Dasiyah already felt like she was Soeraja's sweetheart, but she wasn't sure how he felt about her. So her father's question had clearly struck a nerve.

'So? I'm right, aren't I? That you both are a couple?' Idroes repeated his question, his face stern and his hands folded across his chest.

'Papa, please don't be like this ...'

'I am asking you, Dasiyah, in all seriousness, whether or not you are a couple. You are both joined at the hip, and people see you together all the time. They are starting to ask me about it, and as your father, I don't know how to respond. So, once again, I ask ...' Idroes Moeria began to raise his voice.

'Yes, sir!' Soeraja's voice rang out suddenly. He had regained his composure.

'What?'

'We ... I mean, I ... I have fallen in love with Jeng Yah. But, truthfully, I don't know how she feels about me. All I can do is hope that she also ... Because Jeng Yah is too good to me, I mean, I think she ...' He searched for the right words, and then he tried again, 'I hope she ...' he peeked over at Dasiyah, just for a second, but that was long enough for her to read the pleading request in the young man's eyes. 'I hope that Jeng Yah will accept my love.'

Idroes Moeria was at a loss for words on hearing the raw honesty in the voice of the young man standing before him. The atmosphere grew charged, and he looked at his daughter.

'Yah?' He finally broke the silence between them. 'How about you?'

'I ...' His daughter bowed her head. 'I want to accept Mas Raja's love, Papa.'

And then Idroes Moeria knew that he would have to make a place for the young man in his home and, more so, in his heart.

15

Coconut Hill Cigarettes

Jeng Yah felt like her life was complete. Her business, Lady cigarettes, was advancing and Independence! cigarettes, with its signature red-rolling paper, was still in production. She had a family that loved her, and a sweetheart who was always by her side. She was sure that she would spend the rest of her life with Soeraja. He had earned Idroes Moeria's trust, and the factory business had been duly handed over to him. He was now an overseer, and her father often invited him along to meetings with tobacco and clove wholesalers.

Idroes trusted his daughter's choice. He also liked the young man because he had taken full responsibility for the tasks that had been assigned to him. He was certain that Raja would stay by his daughter's side and become her right-hand man in managing the Lady cigarette factory well into the future.

Unfortunately, Soeraja wasn't so sure. The clever young man indeed adored his sweetheart, and had found some success working for his future father-in-law. But he felt ashamed when, one day, he overheard the conversation between a roller and a trimmer. Neither of them spoke about Soeraja with praise even though he worked hard and managed the factory well – instead they were insulting and derogatory towards him. The issue was that Raja had scolded a trimmer, whose job it was to measure and cut the ends of the cigarettes so they were neat and even, all of the same length. One afternoon, he had measured the lengths of a number of different cigarettes and found one that was longer than the others. He had then scolded the trimmer who had been given the job. He had brandished the ruler and explained its function, insisting that if it wasn't being used to measure a cigarette to its ideal length then it could be used to smack insubordinates. The labourer simply nodded and bowed but after the incident, later in the day, when all the men were standing in line to wash up before prayers and he thought Raja was not around, he grumbled about his boss in Javanese.

'Mas Raja is actually a nobody! He has nothing. Just look, he sleeps at the factory, and if he is hungry he has to ask Bu Roem for food. Pak Idroes is very kind to let him crash here.' The trimmer who had been scolded vented his annoyance to the roller who had witnessed the incident.

The latter replied in Javanese, 'It's true. He was just bumming around looking for work at the night market. He's really lucky that Jeng Yah fell in love with him – if she hadn't, he would still be nothing but a pauper.' The roller nodded as his friend fanned the flames. The two workers gossiped, finishing their ablutions, then left. They didn't realize that Soeraja was standing near the water tap, listening to them. What made him feel worse was that the other workers had heard them talking too, and they also knew Raja was there and had heard it all.

Since then, the young man, who had finally felt well-settled in his life, began to feel unsteady again. He contemplated his long journey as a wanderer. He had experienced hunger, going without food for days, and he had slept by the roadside, under trees, in mosques. He had felt the sting of other people's contempt when they had insulted him for being a vagabond, a beggar. Then, finally, he had found love with Jeng Yah. And love had tamed his spirit, which had been free and independent. Love had made him willing to restrain himself, to sacrifice his physical freedom and stay in one place, to assume all kinds of responsibilities and dedicate himself to any work given to him.

No matter how much Raja wanted to attack those two workers, he controlled himself. He knew that what they had said was right – he was indeed a nobody. In reality, he was merely a man hiding behind the protection and money of his future wife, Jeng Yah. For days, he tried to mask his hurt. And he would have succeeded in doing so for longer if the owner of Coconut Hill cigarettes hadn't come by to see Idroes Moeria. He brought along his son, a young man of twenty-three named Sentot, who had been living in Surabaya while attending university. The city was now spelled 'Surabaya', not 'Soerabaia' as it had been when Idroes was held captive there. A new spelling system had replaced the old Dutch one after Independence, to streamline communication.

Idroes Moeria introduced Sentot to Jeng Yah, and even asked for his daughter to make her special tingwe for the guests. Soeraja, who was busy overseeing the workers, spied on them and tried to eavesdrop on what they were saying. For some reason, he didn't like Sentot. His worries were justified, because a few days later the boy's father returned to see Idroes Moeria again and to announce his son's intentions to propose to Jeng Yah.

The workers were spreading rumours once again, wondering if it were true that Lady cigarettes and Independence! cigarettes would merge with Coconut Hill cigarettes to become a much bigger company. Coconut Hill was a big brand, well known in the cigarette industry for a long time. Idroes Moeria did not immediately respond to Sentot's proposal. He wanted to talk it over with Jeng Yah first. And as secretive as they were about their private conversation, Raja still heard the news, first from the gossip of the workers and then from Rukayah.

'Is it true?'

'It's true, Mas. She has received a proposal.'

'And what will be her answer?'

'I don't know.'

Soeraja quickly took stock of the situation. If the proposal were accepted, he would have to quickly resign from his position as overseer at the factory.

When the owner of Coconut Hill cigarettes came again with Sentot, to ask for Jeng Yah's answer, she politely rejected his proposal and said that her heart belonged to another. Soeraja and Rukayah, who were eavesdropping, smiled at each other when they heard this. After that, Sentot took his leave in a gentlemanly fashion. 'The man Jeng Yah loves is very lucky indeed,' he said.

This incident further convinced Soeraja that he was nothing more than a lucky bastard. Jeng Yah had refused the proposal of a rich man who could help advance her father's business. Whereas Raja, no matter how diligently he devoted himself to Idroes Moeria's company, was still a nobody. So, one afternoon, as he smoked Jeng Yah's tingwe and drank from a cup of tea, he spoke of his desires to Jeng Yah:

'I want to have my own cigarette factory, Jeng.'

Her expression was a mixture of amazement and sadness as she asked, 'Why? Are you not satisfied with your current position here?'

'It's not that, Jeng.' Raja clasped his sweetheart's hands, trying to explain. He hesitated, but finally said, 'I am ashamed.'

'Ashamed of what?' Jeng Yah didn't understand what he meant.

'Ashamed of myself. I'm lying to myself, Jeng. I'm a nobody, but here at this factory I have a position, and have been given power.'

'What do you mean, Mas?'

'All this actually belongs to you, Jeng. It belongs to your father. I'm just a hired supervisor. I'm a nobody.'

'But once we are married, there will be no difference, will there? All of this will belong to you too.'

'And with whose money will we pay for the wedding? Do you want us to just recite our marriage vows and be done with it? Have no celebrations at all?' Jeng Yah was quiet. 'I bet there's no way a prosperous family like yours will want a private wedding. What would people say?'

'Papa can pay for our wedding, Mas.'

'I'm a man, Jeng! There's no way I could do that … Where is my self-respect, my dignity as a man? Now I am working for my future father-in-law, living at my future father-in-law's house, and eating his food too.'

'But that makes sense, Mas. You work here. That's your right as his employee.'

'That's exactly what I'm saying! In other words, I have nothing. I'm a beggar. I'm a big zero, Jeng!'

Dasiyah was sad to hear this come out of the mouth of the man she loved. She had never realized that Raja felt this way.

'I want to have my own cigarette business, Jeng.'

Jeng Yah looked at her future husband, dazed. All of a sudden there were thousands of words at the tip of her tongue, words she couldn't utter because it felt like her mouth was too small and these words too big. Three people passed by the front of their house, handing out political leaflets and screaming out party slogans. Jeng Yah and Raja watched them until they disappeared around the corner. That was enough time for Jeng Yah to gather her thoughts and phrase the words she was holding in her mouth.

'Mas, do you want to leave Lady cigarettes?'

'No, I want to expand this business by merging it with another cigarette line, one that I will start myself.'

She was quiet for a moment. Then she said, 'If that's the case, I can ask Father to give you some start-up money to make – '

'No!' Raja interrupted. He had already anticipated that Jeng Yah would offer him money. 'I don't want to be funded by your family. I want to raise my own money.'

'Are you serious?'

'Yes. I want to prove that I can succeed without your father's help.'

'Mas, why are you being like this all of a sudden? What's really going on?' Jeng Yah still didn't understand.

'I just want to be respected, treated like a real man. Not like a parasite who is living off the generosity of his future in-laws.'

That was the end of the discussion between Soeraja and Jeng Yah. They fell silent. He was sure that if he left to start his own venture, equipped with all of the knowledge he had gained from Idroes Moeria, his future would be bright. But Jeng Yah was sure that if he left, her future, which had just seemed so bright so far, would slip from her grasp.

* * *

Jeng Yah's fears were coming true. It began when Raja asked

Idroes Moeria's permission to seek a future for himself. Unlike Jeng Yah, her father gave him his blessing. The youth continued to live with them and eat his meals at their house, but every day he went out looking for investors who could be convinced to give him some start-up capital. Almost one month passed, and nobody wanted to invest in Raja. It turned out it wasn't as easy as he had imagined it would be.

Soeraja began to worry that his dreams of having his own cigarette business were nothing but hollow fantasies. He also began to feel embarrassed, leaving every morning to find investors, but coming home every afternoon with nothing to show for his efforts. And all the while he was eating and sleeping at the expense of his future father-in-law. One morning, he did not head out. Instead he approached Jeng Yah.

'Can I still help here?'

Jeng Yah smiled brightly; of course he could. That day though, Raja didn't rush to carry out his duties as an overseer like he had before. He was too embarrassed to show his face to the workers.

'Well, if that's how you feel, then you can just work with me, helping me mix the sauce into the tobacco and the cloves. Does that sound good?' Jeng Yah was pleased she could once again enjoy the company of her man.

Raja agreed. He followed Jeng Yah into the back office, which resembled a laboratory, its tables covered with bottles and jars of sauce mixtures. Each bottle emitted its own distinctive aroma. The sauce formulas were written on the wall in chalk, but the only ones who could understand them were Jeng Yah and her father.

Dasiyah returned to relishing the simple joys in life. Here she was once again, doing what she loved, and with the man she loved by her side. Raja helped her pour the sauce mixtures into the bottles, to be sprayed onto the mixture of chopped tobacco and cloves. They blended the sauces for the two different lines, Independence! and Lady.

'The Lady cigarette labels are running out. They will last at most for the next two days,' Jeng Yah said, pointing towards a sheet of neatly arranged Lady cigarette labels.

'Let me go to the printer, Jeng.'

'You don't want me to go with you?'

'There's no need. I can go by myself while you watch over the workers. I ...' Raja tried to gather his thoughts. 'Like I said before, I would feel a bit awkward if I had to supervise the workers now. It feels uncomfortable to have been gone for a whole month and then just suddenly pop up again.' Jeng Yah smiled, understanding her beloved's hesitation.

She agreed to give her man some time to regain his self-confidence. Jeng Yah watched Soeraja go, her heart filling with warm emotion, as warm as an aromatic clove cigarette just born from the hand of a roller.

* * *

Soeraja had gone to the printing press many times before at the behest of Idroes Moeria, and therefore was well-acquainted with Pak Mloyo, the owner of the press. Of course, the owner kept ready a large template for Lady cigarette labels.

Raja looked around at the place. It was lively and loud. The printers operating the press plugged their ears with cotton to diminish the clattering of the machine. Pak Mloyo himself was a bit deaf, and so Raja had to practically scream every time he spoke to him. It was actually a bit exhausting but it was worth it, because Mloyo's work was excellent. He was an expert draftsman and he didn't even charge to draw the image, as long as it was printed at his press.

Soeraja sat facing Pak Mloyo's table, which was crowded with printing paraphernalia: papers, Chinese ink, rulers, compasses, pens, pencils and other kinds of writing and drawing equipment. No one would ever have called his working space neat. In casual Javanese dialect, Pak Mloyo asked Soeraja, shouting, 'How many sheets do you want?'

'Five hundred sheets, Pak.'

'How many?' Pak Mloyo moved his ear closer to Raja, straining to hear.

'Five hundred!' Raja screamed, holding up five fingers.

'Oh, yes, yes ...' Pak Mloyo said and then recorded this on an order form. A worker approached the owner to show him the result of a printed political flier. It seemed to be a proof. 'Like this, sir?' The printer had to shout too. Pak Mloyo examined the work, and then gave a thumbs up. 'Yes!'

The printer yelled out to all his co-workers who were waiting expectantly, 'Yes! That's right! Carry on!'

Raja read the flier as the printer carried it way. It was for the Partai Komunis Indonesia, the Indonesian Communist Party, also known as PKI. He asked the printer, 'This party often makes its fliers here, doesn't it?'

'Very often. It's lot of money! And it's not just fliers – the orders for banners and party flags never stop coming in. If I had to choose, I would choose this party, sir. It's making me rich!' Pak Mloyo explained.

Soeraja fell silent, thinking that this might be an opportunity that he could take advantage of. There was an address written across the bottom of the flier in small print. 'Pak, have you ever been there?' he asked, pointing to the address.

'Of course, I have! That's where I deliver all their orders. They order so many, and sometimes I take them over myself, when no one else is available. Would you like to go there with me?' Raja nodded enthusiastically.

The PKI headquarters was full of energetic folks. Some were gathered in groups, discussing important issues regarding national leaders, and others were going back and forth carrying stacks of fliers, piles of party flags and folded banners. Raja took it all in as he arrived with Pak Mloyo, helping him deliver an order of party flags printed on red cloth. Ever since he had become a regular of the Indonesian Communist Party, Mloyo didn't just receive paper orders but also fabric screen-print orders.

A middle-aged man sat on the edge of a table, facing a group of people who had just arrived. He took out a wad of cash held together with a rubber band and handed the money to those who were asking for it. Raja knew immediately that he was the man in charge. Pak Mloyo got in line, carrying the flags. He stood beside him, taking in the hectic atmosphere around him.

After a few moments, one of the men stepped forward. He instructed all of the party members present there to gather around him.

'Let's just listen to this first. It will only be a moment,' said Pak Mloyo.

Soeraja and he slipped to the back, blending into the group of members. They were all listening attentively, as though they had come here specifically to listen to this speech. A young man, who was much younger than Raja, scrutinized his face.

'You're new, aren't you?' Raja nodded. 'Well, everyone is

welcome.'

'Yes, it's alright. There's no need to worry ...' Pak Mloyo chimed in. It was as if both of them could read the discomfort on Raja's face. He did feel a little ill at ease in the completely unfamiliar environment, but their words calmed him.

'Yes, Pak.'

'Later, I'll introduce you to all the party folks. You have come here regarding setting up a business, haven't you?' Raja nodded. 'I understand. You just have to promise me one thing.'

'What's that, Pak?'

'Don't open a printing press, because then you and I will have to be competitors!' Pak Mloyo chuckled a little. But even though he said like it were a joke, Soeraja knew he was serious.

'Don't worry, Pak. If my proposal is accepted, your business will grow even more because I'll be a regular customer at your press,' Soeraja replied. Pak Mloyo smiled widely at this.

* * *

Raja went home after nightfall. He found Jeng Yah waiting in front of the house, along with Idroes Moeria.

'Ah, there he is!' she said. She seemed worried about her fiancée.

Raja sat down next to Idroes Moeria while Jeng Yah hurried to fetch him some water. But he asked for her to come back and said he wasn't thirsty, 'Stay here a moment, Jeng. I want to tell you something.' So she sat down in the shadows.

'I just met with someone, and it looks like he might be able to give me some money.'

Idroes replied enthusiastically, 'Oh really? Wow, that's great!'

Jeng Yah, on the other hand, didn't like this news at all. 'So you didn't go order the labels, but instead went looking for an investor, is that it?'

'Hey, I took care of the labels first! They will be ready in a week.'

Jeng Yah turned away, annoyed.

'So who wants to give you the start-up money?' Idroes asked eagerly.

'It's not confirmed yet that he wants to, sir. I still have to get to know him a little bit. I can't rush in thoughtlessly ... I can't just ask for money without getting acquainted with the man first.'

'Oh yes, of course, you're right!' Idroes was still enthusiastic.

'So, in the next couple of weeks I will go see him again. Who knows, perhaps he will come to trust me.' As Raja spoke with hope, Jeng Yah's heart sank. She was afraid he was distancing himself from her once again.

Idroes Moeria nodded. He completely understood Raja's feelings – in fact, the young man's situation reminded him of his own, and the way he had first started his own cigarette company for Roemaisa. He felt as if he was seeing a young version of himself in his future son-in-law.

Soeraja, who only a few days ago had been intending to return to his work as overseer at Lady cigarettes, had changed his plans again. Now every morning, after helping Jeng Yah mix the sauces into the chopped tobacco and cloves, he rushed off to his new activities. Usually, he went to Pak Mloyo's place first, offering to bring the previous day's orders to the PKI headquarters, which gave him a chance to grow close to the party members.

Soon after this new routine began, Jeng Yah looked disturbed, as if dark storm clouds had settled over her face.

Raja tried to reassure her. 'I'm positive, Jeng, that this time I will get some start-up investment. These party members have a lot of money. They order piles and piles of banners and flags!' Jeng Yah stared at Soeraja as he spoke excitedly. Then she ignored him and started pouring out the mixed sauce into the spray bottles. 'Here, Jeng, let me help ...'

'I don't need your help!' Her voice came out with such angry force, she herself was surprised by it.

'Hey, what's wrong, Jeng? Are you angry with me?'

'What do you think? I don't want you to leave. I want you here by my side, taking care of Lady cigarettes!' She burst into tears. 'If you go, Mas Raja, I'm worried that you will return to your old life – free and unbound, going anywhere you please, to any city you want, with no one to take care of you, and with no one for you to care about. You will not have to take care of Lady cigarettes or me. You can do whatever you want. And then you will forget all about me.' Dasiyah sobbed uncontrollably. A few of the workers passing by witnessed the drama.

'Jeng?' Raja had never guessed that his beloved felt so strongly about this. He approached her, but the girl pushed him and moved away. Finally, Raja simply took the bottle and left the room, heading to spray the chopped tobacco and cloves with flavouring. He worked in silence, and the workers helping him were also quiet, even though they were gesturing to each other wordlessly that their boss was out of sorts because of a lover's spat with Jeng Yah. Raja chose to let her be, so she could cry as much as she wanted. He sprayed the two different sauces from their spray bottles for Independence! and Lady cigarettes respectively.

When he returned to the back office, Raja's beloved was not there. He looked for Jeng Yah everywhere, but could not find her at the factory or at the house. Perhaps she had gone out to try and calm her thoughts? He realized he had to give his sweetheart some more time to be alone and reconcile. That day, Raja did not go to the party headquarters. He waited for Jeng Yah on the house's terrace with Idroes Moeria.

'Don't worry. That's just how women are. They are difficult to understand.' Idroes tried to comfort Soeraja with a few trite phrases. They tried to think of where Jeng Yah might have gone.

'I'm going to go now, sir. I want to look for Jeng Yah,' Soeraja eventually said.

'Alright. Be careful.' Idroes shook his head, amused by their young love.

Raja found her in the storehouse where the newly bought tobacco was stored in the shape of giant spindles. She was sitting behind a big bale of tobacco, smoking. The storehouse had a high roof, and the aroma of tobacco was free to waft away in the air and drift up to the rooftops. Soeraja had always known how much Jeng Yah loved clove cigarettes, and perhaps that was why he had suddenly realized he might find her here.

'I know you are angry with me, Jeng. I know you'd prefer it if I just stayed with you. But if I stay here with you forever, then what will become of me?'

'You don't want to be by my side?'

'That's not what I mean. It's precisely because I want to become a suitable companion and partner to you and want to be able to support you – and want you to be proud of me – that I have to do this.' Jeng Yah stared at Soeraja.

'Even though you didn't tell me about the proposal from the son of the Coconut Hill cigarettes' owner, I know about it,' he confessed.

Now Jeng Yah's look changed to one of surprise. 'Who told you? It was Rukayah, wasn't it?'

'Rukayah didn't have to say anything. All the workers knew about it. I do have ears, don't I, Jeng?'

'But if that's the case, then you must know that I refused him too.'

'I know. And that made me feel even more ashamed! You chose me, which means that you must value me highly, even though I am a nobody. But I have to be able to stand on my own two feet and prove that I am worthy of your love. I will certainly return to you, Jeng. I'm already tired of wandering, moving from one city to the next. My home is here with you.'

She embraced him. 'Do you promise, Mas, that you will always come home to me?'

'I promise.'

For two months after that, Soeraja went to the PKI house almost every day. Everyone there grew familiar with him, so he didn't need Pak Mloyo to accompany him anymore. Then, one day, he finally came home with feelings of joy, rather than ones of inadequacy. He had finally been given some money to make a new brand of cigarettes. He enthusiastically recounted how he had pitched his idea and spoken convincingly about why the party should invest in his clove cigarettes:

'These days everyone smokes cloves, right? Just imagine this ... Everyone who buys my cigarettes will automatically come to know about the PKI party. Furthermore, we all know that if someone likes a particular brand of cigarettes, they keep buying them. So, spending money on these cigarettes is an investment – it's money that will come back to the party as people buy more and more packs. It's even better than spending money on banners or flags, which are used only once before being thrown away.' Jeng Yah was overjoyed to see how eagerly her man was recounting it all to her. 'They even gave me a space where I could roll the cigarettes, Jeng. It's indeed true that the party has a lot of money!'

'Well, Mas, are you going to tell me what your cigarettes will be called?'

'I am going with the name the party has requested for my brand … Red Sickle cigarettes.'

16

Smoke Red Sickle Cigarettes

It was a memorable day for Soeraja when he started making his Red Sickle cigarettes. It was the first time he was making something he could call his own. His heart had been overjoyed when his pitch to the PKI party was successful. The party had given him a fair amount of money after being reassured that a cigarette line was an effective tool for spreading their political propaganda. After all, cigarettes have the power to make someone feel loyal – if someone likes a certain brand, then he will return to it again and again, and he will certainly remember the image on the label. So all one had to do was make a cigarette that people would enjoy. Moreover, cigarettes weren't like the other forms of propaganda, such as banners or political fliers. Those didn't return their investment, because they were made, disseminated, read, and then thrown away. But their investment in clove cigarettes, if they planned it right, would return to them quickly. They had to only ensure that the launching and dissemination of the product was well planned. Soeraja already had the idea to introduce his cigarettes through political fliers; he would stamp on them the logo of his Red Sickle brand. Anyone faithful to the PKI party would most certainly try the cigarettes and, if they were lucky, those who liked smoking them would keep on buying them.

Soeraja had already left Independence! and Lady cigarettes,

as well as given up his lodging at Idroes Moeria's. The PKI party had given him enough money to rent a house, and he used this accommodation to manufacture his cigarettes as well. Workers gathered there to roll, trim and pack Red Sickle cigarettes. Now Soeraja only went over to his in-laws' house once in a while, on weekends, to visit Jeng Yah. He was incredibly proud that he was finally independent, without being supported by his future father-in-law.

Six months after he felt truly settled, Raja gathered up the courage to propose to Jeng Yah officially. He came over to her house one day, looking neater and more dressed up than usual. He expressed his intentions to marry Dasiyah and take her for his wife. Of course, Idroes Moeria and his wife Roemaisa happily accepted his proposal.

'Sir, I would also like to set the date,' he said. Jeng Yah beamed, and her cheeks blushed red. Rukayah, her younger sister, nudged her arm playfully, just as happy about Soeraja's request.

'Yes, yes, yes …' Idroes Moeria went to fetch the calendar.

'Let's not wait too long,' Soeraja urged, and again Jeng Yah blushed.

'Yes, but let's not rush either. A wedding reception takes some time to prepare for,' Roemaisa answered. Idroes returned with the calendar, and his wife leaned in to get a better look. He was holding a calendar for the year 1965.

'Do you want to have the wedding this year?'

'Yes, it has to be this year, sir. Next year is too late.'

Raja was really eager, Idroes Moeria could see that. 'How about October? Is four months enough time to prepare, Bu?' he asked his wife.

Roemaisa smiled. 'Yes. We will ensure it is enough time. We

can make it work.'

'Yes, Pak, Bu, that date is just fine,' Soeraja confirmed. After that, he gave Jeng Yah a golden bracelet. 'This October, I will wed you with a ring,' he whispered as he fastened the clasp around her wrist.

* * *

Jeng Yah prepared for her wedding celebrations with great excitement. She wanted to wear a Javanese-lace kebaya blouse with black velvet trim as her wedding dress, and a formal bun in her hair, and slippers embellished with little decorative beads on her feet. She imagined herself standing with her new husband by her side, surrounded by guests, thanking them one by one for coming. She already had a number of dishes in mind for the reception menu: sambel goreng ati with chillies and chicken liver; rissoles; soup; creamy pineapple-flavoured es puter for dessert. She tried out the recipes herself, cooking them to ensure that there were no mistakes with the flavours. She had also contacted a wedding makeup specialist, someone who was older and had a warm and orderly household, and enjoyed a faithful and lasting marriage with her husband. She had already asked politely that the woman fast for seven days before the big event, so that everything would go smoothly and the aura around the bride and groom would be radiant. Jeng Yah had already thought everything through, and she had made preparations to the very last detail.

If only the plans hadn't remained merely that. If only their world hadn't been turned upside down by savage hate, and if only the following people had never died: General Achmad Yani, Major General M.T. Harjono, Major General S. Parman, Major General

Suprapto, Brigadier General D.I. Pandjaitan, Brigadier General Sutojo Siswomihardjo, Second Inspector Karel Satsuit Tubun, First Lieutenant Pierre Tendean, Colonel Sugiono and Brigadier General Katamso Darmokusumo. If only these men hadn't been suspected of being murdered as part of a Communist plot to overthrow the country, then that never would have become a reason for the destruction of the Communist party. And if all this had not happened, then Soeraja never would have been in danger of losing his life. He had become closely affiliated with the PKI party after all, because he made cigarettes called Red Sickle and his brand had been funded by the Indonesian Communist Party. And if Soeraja hadn't had to flee from M Town to save his life, the wedding plans of the cigarette girl never would have been ruined.

One night some of Soeraja's acquaintances were found floating in Pepe River, murdered, and he realized that his life was in danger too. He snuck out in secret to the Red Sickle cigarette factory and found it completely empty. All the labourers had already fled for their lives. He took a pile of unused labels that he had been saving in the office and burned them. He was aware that this was probably pointless; Red Sickle cigarettes had been available in the market for quite a while now, which meant he was already known as the brand's producer. But Soeraja was desperate and was feeling like a madman. Meanwhile, a death squad had established itself in their city. And no longer were its members covertly slaughtering those involved with the PKI and throwing them into Pepe River before dawn; instead, in broad daylight, they were banging on the front doors of people who had been involved with the PKI. Just as Soeraja was trying to burn the rest of the chopped tobacco that was neatly stocked in the Red Sickle factory, he saw an armed mob heading for his factory.

Soeraja slipped outside, running into the bamboo thicket. He made his way through the underbrush to Jeng Yah's place, hoping he could see her and say goodbye, but when he arrived at the rice fields in front of her house, he saw that the mob was already banging on her door, screaming and carrying torches. When Idroes Moeria, his future father-in-law, opened the door, a member of the mob shoved him to the ground with full force. Soeraja immediately abandoned his plan. He hid for a while in the mounds of rice paddy and wet mud, and then, covered in muck, he slipped away.

He was lucky that he obeyed the inner voice that had told him to get away quickly. If not, he surely would have joined the bodies floating dead in Pepe River. But as he ran to make his escape, he never stopped thinking about Jeng Yah and what he had witnessed that night – the mob of people forcing themselves into her home and knocking his future father-in-law down. The mob had come to their house because they knew Soeraja had lived there and had a special relationship with Jeng Yah. How he longed to leave a letter for his sweetheart, to tell her how he was doing. Jeng must be very worried about him, he thought. But he knew that wouldn't be a wise thing to do – he could be traced through the letter and might find himself in mortal danger. But he regretted not having had the chance to say goodbye to her, and that he had been forced to disappear from her life suddenly, as if swallowed by the earth.

Jeng Yah was in shock. She felt like a distraught dove that has lost its mate. It was three weeks before the day of their wedding, but Soeraja was gone, and M Town was dark, the dead floating in Pepe River. Its waters were no longer filled with fish and crawfish, but only human remains.

Jeng Yah was indicted because of a silly coincidence. When the National Armed Forces, the Tentara Nasional Indonesia or TNI, arrived, they didn't just rummage through the PKI headquarters, they also captured people who were somehow involved with or had links to the party. They stormed the press where the PKI ordered the printing of their propaganda material, and this was the same press where the Red Sickle cigarette labels were printed, and also where the invitations to Dasiyah and Soeraja's wedding were printed. That press belonged to none other than Pak Mloyo. Raja had wanted the invitations printed there because he knew Pak Mloyo well and was therefore given a special discount.

Soeraja often wondered how Pak Mloyo was fairing. It would be a miracle if he had survived; it was more likely that he had been tossed into Pepe River. Perhaps Raja had seen his corpse already but hadn't recognized him amongst the others, or perhaps the man lay buried at the bottom of the river, under a pile of other corpses.

The TNI had stormed Idroes Moeria's house with a mob of people who supported the destruction of the PKI party, and had captured Jeng Yah and her father. The girl was arrested because of her romantic relationship with Soeraja, and her father was arrested for giving his blessing to Jeng Yah's relationship with a Communist. During her capture, the troops had found and thrown to the floor a sack of wedding invitations, and as the family had looked on, they told Jeng Yah that this was proof of her involvement with a Communist. The girl was trapped, even though she had never even set foot in the PKI headquarters of M Town. Idroes was in more trouble because they had discovered that he made Independence! cigarettes, which used red cigarette paper, the colour that was now associated with the PKI party and the blood of the murdered generals, who were believed to be victims of an attempted Communist coup. Idroes Moeria never would have guessed that the nightmare of the Japanese occupation, the nightmare he had locked up tight inside him twenty years ago, would return to haunt him again during his twilight years. His arrest and torture in TNI custody unlocked a flood of repressed pain and bad memories.

Their luck changed in prison though, once their captors realized that Jeng Yah was the cigarette girl of Lady cigarettes, the woman whose spit was as sweet as Roro Mendut's. A strong young man in uniform appeared to guard the father and daughter. This wasn't his official duty – in fact, it was sheer coincidence that he happened to be there. He scrutinized the faces of the prisoners, and as the young sergeant's gaze fell on Jeng Yah's face, he ordered for his subordinates to bring her to the interrogation room.

Jeng Yah was prepared to die. She had surrendered to whatever fate awaited her. She had already let go of her dread and fear. But then the young sergeant asked her to take a good look at him.

'Do you remember me?' he asked.

At first Jeng Yah was silent, but then she remembered him. 'Sentot?'

He was the suitor she had once refused, the son of the Coconut Hill cigarette owner, who had asked for her hand in marriage. He had joined the TNI.

'Are you a Communist, Jeng?'

Jeng Yah shook her head. 'No,' she insisted. Tears slid out of her eyes.

Sentot took out an envelope. 'Would you like a cigarette?' he offered. She opened the envelope and found inside some rolling paper, chopped cloves and tobacco. She inhaled the aroma of the tobacco, and for a moment was comforted by its familiar smell.

'You don't smoke Coconut Hill cigarettes?' she asked.

'Would you believe it if I said that I can't smoke my father's kretek anymore?'

'Why not?'

Sentot chuckled, feeling shy and a bit reluctant to answer Jeng Yah's question. 'The day I proposed to you, your father offered me a tingwe that he said you had rolled.'

'Yes, indeed. I rolled it over a number of days. First I took the tobacco residue that was stuck to my hands and then mixed it with chopped cloves and srinthil. Then I rolled it myself. And then I sealed the paper with my spit.'

'That's it ... Since then I haven't been able to smoke anything else.'

Jeng Yah couldn't believe her ears. 'What do you mean?'

'I knew there was no way I could get your tingwe, except from you directly. So I tried to trick my own senses instead, by rolling kretek on my own to smoke, all the while hoping that it would taste like the one I had sampled at your house.'

Jeng Yah smiled at this. She opened the envelope again and rolled a tingwe for him. She sealed the paper with her tongue. 'Here,' she said, handing Sentot the cigarette. 'To ease your longing just a bit.' He smiled as he accepted it. He drew out a lighter and quickly lit the end of the tingwe.

Jeng Yah said, 'The taste must be slightly different, because the tingwe I usually make has to go through a fairly long process. I need a day of rolling, so that I can gather the kretek residue that sticks to the palms of my hands. And the sauce mixture I use is key to its delicious taste.'

'Yes, it's slightly different, but it is enough to soothe my longing for your kretek.' Jeng Yah let Sentot smoke the clove undisturbed. Then, when he was finished, Sentot spoke again, 'If you had agreed to marry me back then, you wouldn't be in this situation now.'

'I know.'

'Do you regret it?'

'No. Because I have found true love,' Jeng Yah replied.

'Oh, yes. A love that has gone missing suddenly now ... He's the guy who makes Red Sickle cigarettes, isn't he, this love of yours?'

Jeng Yah's eyes welled up, and tears streamed down her cheeks.

'I believe you,' Sentot said suddenly.

'What do you believe?' she asked, confused.

'I believe that you are not a Communist. You are just a girl in love who has found herself in an unfortunate situation. I will help you get out of here. Do as I say, alright?'

She gaped at him for a moment in disbelief. Then she nodded her assent.

Sentot introduced Jeng Yah to the other TNI troops as the 'cigarette girl', and she rolled a few tingwe for them. He explained to them that Independence! cigarettes had no relationship whatsoever with the PKI party, and that the company was started years ago and named out of respect for Soekarno, who had proclaimed independence. The red colour they had chosen for the paper was taken from the national flag, the Red and White, and it symbolized courage. That was the concept behind Independence! cigarettes, a product that had been intended to rekindle the courage and spirit of the people and help them win their freedom from foreign occupation.

It was a miracle: exactly one day before the scheduled date of Jeng Yah's wedding to Soeraja, she and Idroes Moeria were set free. Meanwhile, Rukayah had been walking up and down the banks of Pepe River to see whether she would find the bodies of her father and her older sister floating there. Upon his release, Idroes was forbidden from selling Independence! cigarettes. The Lady cigarette line was allowed to continue production, however. Jeng Yah was further advised to bury the name Soeraja deep in her heart, and go on living as if she had never known him nor had any kind of relationship, let alone a romance, with him. When they were released, the soldiers told her not to waste her blessing, of being the incarnation of Roro Mendut.

It was true that Jeng Yah had been absolved from the allegations of her involvement with Communists and she had returned home a free woman. But as she stepped out of her captivity, it only took her a moment to discover that her heart, which had been burning so far with a strong and steady flame, was now frozen and left without feeling. Her love had been smothered lifeless by destiny, and there was nothing left of her wedding plans now but her fantasies. Jeng Yah realized that she and Soeraja would never be together. And what hurt most of all was that she still hadn't heard any word from her man, and she didn't even know whether he was alive or dead.

Idroes Moeria, who had been granted his freedom after being imprisoned for the second time in his life, was not as happy as he should have been at regaining his independence. Unlike twenty years ago, when he had returned from the Japanese prison, he was no longer young. At the time, he had his whole life before him, and one thousand reasons to begin again and rebuild from the rubble the life the Japanese had destroyed – but not this time. Now, he was old, too exhausted to feel excited. He felt fortunate just to be alive, and he had no strength left to build anything new. Independence! cigarettes had been his life for decades. And now his kretek had been banned for a ridiculous reason. Gradually, the man's health began to decline. He wept every time he saw the Independence! labels stocked around his home, waiting to be stuck onto a pack before being sent out into the world. His wife Roemaisa was forced to gather up all these labels and hide them just to preserve her husband's sanity. Even though Lady cigarettes could still be produced and sold, for months there was no real business activity. The political situation made it difficult, and the people seemed lost and defeated suddenly, as if they had lost their spirit too on the night their fellow townsfolk had been killed and thrown into the river. Even those who were truly and completely uninvolved with Communism were afraid of being implicated. Moreover, cigarettes were not the foremost thought on people's minds. Everyone was just trying to survive. Idroes Moeria's entire extended family was in hibernation, making the wise decision to lay low and live off their savings.

* * *

As for the man in exile, Soeraja, he was still terrified. He walked around with a thick beard and dressed in filthy clothes, fearful of losing his life. He had seen his friends from M Town's PKI headquarters murdered. He decided to go as far away as he could, and distance himself from Jeng Yah. He just wanted to disappear and to ensure that his beloved was in no way involved with him, so that she could survive. He didn't even risk sending her a letter.

One day, when he grew tired of being on the run and of longing for Jeng Yah, he followed his nose to a place that reminded him of her: a tobacco storehouse. He took a pinch of tobacco from one of the bales piled in tall stacks that reached up to the ceiling. He remembered how Jeng Yah had taught him to tell the difference between good and bad tobacco.

'You could be completely blind and it wouldn't matter, but your sense of smell and touch have to work together to judge the tobacco,' she had said. Soeraja remembered how his beloved would close her eyes while her nimble fingers pulled out a handful of tobacco and brought it to her nose. She would inhale the tobacco's fragrance to discern if it was good. Soeraja now did the same thing. As the aroma of the tobacco entered his nostrils, it was as if his cigarette girl had been returned to him and was standing right before him. The door to the storehouse was open, and suddenly she appeared in the doorway, surrounded by sunlight. He could almost touch her. Her supple, voluptuous figure seemed to beckon him to her. He squinted at the storehouse door, as the light surrounding the silhouette made his vision blur. The youth emerged from his hiding place. He was sure that the silhouette belonged to Jeng Yah. His beloved had come to him. She had found him. But as he moved closer, and as his vision cleared, he saw it was someone else. The woman was not Jeng Yah. She was not his cigarette girl.

'Who are you?' she asked him fearfully. Soeraja stared vacantly in her direction. He felt a pang of regret.

'Pur, who is it?' Suddenly he heard another voice; the deep voice of a man.

'Father, there is someone here!' the girl called back to him.

The man appeared before Soeraja, also just a silhouette at

first. Soeraja tried to clear his vision again. But for some reason, this time his eyes did not respond. In fact, the beams of light just got brighter. Soeraja fell down in a sudden faint.

When he came to, he found himself sitting in a room. He could clearly see the face of the girl, called Pur, and the man she had called her father. He tried to hone his memory, because he was sure that a few months ago he had met this girl in M Town. At the time, Jeng Yah had introduced her as the daughter of one of their competitors. He realized the girl before him was Purwanti, the eldest daughter of Pak Djagad, the owner of Proclamation cigarettes and Djagad cloves.

Out of pity for the poor stranger, Pak Djagad decided to help Soeraja. He could imagine what the young man had been through – after all, he himself had been distraught to see the human remains floating in Pepe River and had decided to move away to Kudus. He allowed the young man to live in his factory. At first, Soeraja was just a security guard. Then he worked as a roller, making cigarettes for Djagad cloves. Then he became a supervisor, assuming the position of trust and responsibility with great ease. Pak Djagad took a liking to Soeraja and was impressed with his knowledge about kretek. Djagad's daughter Purwanti reminded Soeraja of Jeng Yah. Although she was slightly younger and didn't have the passion for kretek that his beloved did, the fact that she was the child of a cigarette-factory owner reminded Soeraja of his deep longing for Jeng Yah. Although Soeraja had no intention of stealing Purwanti's heart, the girl, without realizing it, had already fallen in love with him. She admired his hard work and dedication.

Purwanti was the eldest of five children, and she had two sisters and two brothers. The boys were still quite young and couldn't really help in any way with the cigarette business. So she was happy that Soeraja was there by her father's side, because Djagad finally had someone who could be relied upon to take care of the company's dealings. Even though she herself had grown up around cigarettes her whole life and knew a thing or two about kretek, she acknowledged that she didn't have an exceptional gift for running the business.

Soeraja was spending so much time in Purwanti's company that she soon found herself unable to take her eyes off him. After a while, she came to understand why her acquaintance Jeng Yah in M Town was so attracted to Mas Raja, which is what Pur called him. When Raja told her all about how he missed Jeng Yah and how worried he was about her condition, at first Purwanti listened with patience, but then one day she responded harshly: 'I have heard all these stories already. Now please be quiet, because I am bored of them, and I don't want to hear any more. Besides, even if I wanted to, I would never be able to tell you so freely about the man I have fallen in love with.'

'Pur, forgive me. I didn't know you felt that way. But you can tell me anything. Whom do you love?'

'No, I can't!'

'Why not? Tell me!' Soeraja smiled, gazing at Purwanti. The girl remained mute and not a word came out of her mouth. But her eyes spoke enough. She looked at his face, holding back tears, and after a brief moment she turned and left. And that was when Soeraja realized that the girl had fallen in love with him.

* * *

Soeraja was aware that he had to conduct himself properly with

Pur and respect her feelings – after all, she was the daughter of his boss. He never again mentioned Jeng Yah's name. He kept his overwhelming longing for his beloved buried deep inside himself. He wanted to restore his relationship with Purwanti. But after a while, the girl took Soeraja's silence to mean his consent for her romantic feelings, and believed he was giving her permission to love him – and what man would not yield if he were showered with the kind of indulgent attention Purwanti gave Soeraja constantly. The youth began to compare his beloved, who was so far away, to the sweet girl right in front of him, who was so crazy about him. Finally, when he felt the situation was safe enough, he emboldened himself to send Jeng Yah a letter using a fake name. At first he just wanted to let her know that he was all right, and ask how she was doing. After he was satisfied that Jeng Yah had told him everything about what had happened to her and Idroes when they had been briefly detained, Soeraja changed the topic of conversation: he confessed to her that he had a new sweetheart.

Purwanti didn't know about these letters. But then, one day, Soeraja kissed her, and afterwards he admitted to her that he still was exchanging letters with Jeng Yah. The girl sulked, as he had expected. She was quite sensitive and emotional when it came to dealing with her problems. Purwanti then gave him an ultimatum: Raja had to choose between her and Jeng Yah.

The day she challenged Soeraja to make his choice was the day Pak Djagad called on him for a talk, man-to-man rather than as boss-to-employee. During their conversation, Raja was overcome with a feeling of déjà vu. The typical questions of a concerned father, about whether his intentions towards his daughter were serious and honourable, were once again posed to him. He felt like he was in a dream as he listened to Pak Djagad: the words were exactly what Moeria had said to him only months ago. And Soeraja himself still cherished the same ambition: he wanted to have his own cigarette company, so that he wasn't completely dependent on his father-in-law. Or at least he didn't want to be thought of as living off of his wealthy in-laws. He didn't want to merely stand in their shadow.

But this time, Soeraja's skills and his knowledge about kretek made him very valuable to Pak Djagad. Raja should have thanked Jeng Yah and Idroes Moeria, who had taught him everything he knew. He was deemed fit to enter into an equal partnership with Pak Djagad, and the name Djagad kretek was changed to Djagad Raja kretek. Moreover, and this was most important to Soeraja, Pak Djagad, with his influence as the owner of a successful and popular cigarette business, had enough money and clout to get him a new identity card that would be free of the dreaded 'OT' designation. The two letters indicated that the bearer of the card had been involved with an organisasi terlarang, or a forbidden organization. Of course, this card was of utmost importance to Pak Djagad as well. The young man was going to marry his daughter, and if 'OT' was stamped on his identity card, then the family name and the Djagad clove cigarette name would certainly become tainted too, and that might destroy his business. And when people began to catch on to Soeraja's secret past, Pak Djagad swiftly shut the mouths of anyone who intended to smear his future son-in-law's name. As if it were duct tape, he used money to close their lips tightly. Raja was truly a lucky bastard.

16

Djagad

'Do you remember, Bas, when we spent our vacation at our grandfather's house in M Town? Father took Mas Tegar to Temanggung during the school break, and I was heartbroken because I wanted to go along too, so then we all went to M Town.' Karim glanced at Lebas through the rear-view mirror. It looked like he was dozing off in the backseat; his eyes were open just a crack and then fell close again. Or perhaps he was just pretending to be asleep.

'M Town is in between Yogyakarta and Magelang. There is only one main road that runs through it. Really, only one! That's it! It's an odd little town,' Karim continued, as if he didn't care if anyone was listening to him. He was in a good mood, happy to be away from the factory routine for a while.

The last time Karim had gone on a road trip like this was a month before his wedding. He had driven to Las Vegas from Los Angeles. Before the trip, he had been able to visit Lebas, who had been studying in San Francisco. He had arrived at the college to find that his kid brother had turned into a Bob Marley fanatic and had completely shaved his head.

The trip to Vegas with his friends had been an unforgettable experience. He hadn't really intended to have a bachelor party even though he was set to get married in a month. But as soon as they had arrived in Vegas, Karim's friends had surprised him with one anyway. And you know what they said about Vegas: what happens in Vegas, stays in Vegas. Nobody would have ever believed that Karim had a bachelor party anyway, because that sort of thing was 'not Karim'. Lebas, perhaps, would do such a thing; he was free-spirited, and his two older brothers were secretly jealous of this. But Tegar would never have a bachelor party; he was too strict and stayed away from anything like that.

'Will it take us a long time to reach there? Where are we?' Lebas murmured groggily, waking up. He had risen early that morning to avoid getting splashed with a bucket full of cold water. Tegar certainly would have followed through on his threat, especially with him.

'All you do is sleep!' Tegar grumbled.

'If you want to sleep, you can too, you know? It's not forbidden.'

'What! How dare you ...' Tegar's voice rose suddenly.

'Enough! Enough! Stop making a fuss! You're both grown up but you still fight like kids. It blows my mind.' Since Karim has been fated to be born as the middle child, it had become his duty to mediate between them. 'We really should be concerned here.'

'Concerned ... You are always concerned about something,' Lebas whispered petulantly under his breath. Karim really was 'concerned' quite often.

'Yes, I am concerned!' Karim practically shouted. Then he pulled over in one decisive swerve. The car came to a rest on the hard shoulder.

'Why are you stopping?' his elder brother protested.

'If you two can't get along, then I am turning around and going back to Jakarta. I swear, I will!' Karim threatened.

'You're acting silly. How would you even get there?'

'I'll take the bus!' Karim got out of the car and went to stand by the roadside, waiting for the next bus – any bus that might take him to a terminal where he could find a connection back to Jakarta.

'Mas Karim!' Lebas got out too, trying to calm his brother. 'Mas, come on, get back in the car.'

'Kowe wae terusno kono! Aku wes bosen nengahi kalian! You guys are always like this ... I'm sick of being stuck in the middle.' When he got angry, Karim's Javanese always came out. He was fed up of having to play the mediator.

'Koyok cah cilik wae kowe,' Tegar grumbled back in Javanese: You're acting like a kid. He stayed in the car, arguing through the open passenger window.

'I don't care!'

Tegar snorted, watching Lebas trying to convince Karim to come back. But to no avail. The latter remained adamant. Finally, Tegar got out of the car. Then, he extended his hand towards Lebas. The latter couldn't believe his eyes. 'Seriously, Mas?'

'What do you think?'

Karim would never have guessed that Tegar would be the one to declare a truce. Lebas moved to shake his brother's hand, but then he stopped and held out just his pinky instead. Teasingly, he wiggled his finger like he was a kid making up after a small squabble. After making a show of turning away, Tegar agreed eventually. He held out his own little finger and linked it with Lebas's. They made up. Karim smiled.

'Okay, are you satisfied now?' Tegar asked. Karim's smile grew wider. He realized that this moment ought to be preserved forever. It was not every day, after all, that his two brothers pinky-promised to be friends.

'Yes, I'm satisfied. But it's your turn to drive now ... Okay, Bas?' Karim got in the backseat of the car, and was followed by Tegar, who sat in the passenger seat.

'But I'm still sleepy,' Lebas protested.

'That's exactly why I'm asking. You must drive so you'll be forced to wake up a little. I'll tell you some good stories on our way there, and you won't feel sleepy anymore.'

'Will you tell me the story of *Kancil Nyolong Timun*? How Kancil, the clever little mouse deer, stole a cucumber from the farmer?'

'I don't want to tell you a children's story! I'll tell you the story of our Grandfather Djagad. I'm sure you haven't heard it yet.'

Lebas climbed in the driver's seat. He started the car. And Karim began. As they drove on, he told his brothers everything he knew about their family and the Djagad Raja clove cigarette dynasty. It all had started with their grandfather ...

* * *

'His full name was Soedjagad. It is said that in the old times, people could choose their own names once they were old enough. Grandfather Djagad wasn't born with the name Soedjagad. "Soe" meant "sumber", or source, and "Djagad" meant "dunia", or world. That was quite a name – a heavy-duty name indeed. But he was actually born with a modest name, as simple as a prayer: Uripno. In Javanese, "urip" is life, and the suffix "no" means "kan", or to give. Uripno meant to give life. He was born a small, weak baby, and had almost died from malnutrition.

'Uripno's father was a poor farm worker. Soon after he was born, famine struck M Town. It is said that golden snails attacked the plants, almost like in a fairytale. But unlike in those stories, food did not then magically appear on their tables. Instead, the people found that all their fields had turned pink because the snails had mated and laid their eggs on almost every single stalk of germinated rice, shrivelling them and killing the grains inside. Of course, their harvest failed.

'Uripno's father decided to leave the fields and quit his profession as farmer. He began working for Kyai Idris, who owned a shoe business in M Town's market. He didn't realize it then but this was an excellent decision, because he would soon become Kyai Idris's right-hand man. Uripno was the eldest amongst eight siblings. And as he grew into a young man, he decided to help his parents by becoming a cigarette roller at Pak Trisno's place.

'Growing up, he had a friend called Idroes. But just as Uripno entered his adolescence and decided to change his name to Soedjagad, the friendship between the two boys underwent a rift, and it was all because of a woman called Roemaisa. She was close to Soedjagad, and in fact they were almost married. But then things didn't work out, because Idroes Moeria stole her.'

'How do you know this story?' Tegar asked.

'Grandfather Djagad told it to me himself,' Karim answered.

Karim wasn't the golden child whom their father had taken along to Temanggung and other cities to hunt for tobacco, and he had not been handed the secret recipe for the Djagad Raja kretek sauce, nor was he the son who didn't care about the family business but preferred to dabble in the arts and stay as far away from home as possible. No, Karim was the son who liked to listen, and he paid close attention to whoever and whatever was in front of him. So while Tegar was being groomed to become the next leader of Djagad Raja, and while Lebas was running away to play with this friends, Karim had stayed at home and listened to Grandfather Djagad tell his stories. And this made him fall in love with Djagad Raja in a very special way. He knew its roots, and he had always felt that knowing this history would be useful to him some day, although he wasn't sure in what way exactly. Perhaps, for instance, it might just be useful in helping him entertain his two brothers on a long drive to M Town. Karim continued his story ...

* * *

'Roemaisa was the daughter of the town scribe. The man had ordered shoes from Djagad's father on a number of occasions. In fact, those shoes hadn't been made for him, but for the Dutch, the scribe's employers. But Djagad was told to deliver the shoes to the scribe's house, and there he had seen Roemaisa for the first time.

'Djagad had decided to ask for her hand. But he soon realized he wasn't the only one to want her – it turned out that there were many other young men who also fancied Roemaisa. He wasn't too surprised about this though, considering that she was such a sweet and beautiful girl who was just coming into her own. But what he really couldn't bear was that even his childhood friend, Idroes Moeria, felt the same way about her. So Djagad went as quickly as he could to propose to Roemaisa. He thought that if he did that, he would be regarded as a confident man with serious intentions about her. But then, it turned out that he was rejected. And for what seemed to him like a silly reason: because Djagad couldn't read or write. He had even taken along a pair of high-quality shoes for the scribe. Usually only Dutch men wore such good shoes; they weren't cheap, and they could only be bought with gulden. But even after he had offered the expensive gift to the scribe, he had been rejected, and only because he was illiterate. He couldn't believe that he had been sent away for such a flimsy reason.

'For a while, Djagad had assumed that Roemaisa would regret the decision and reconsider his proposal. But, he was left completely shocked to discover that Idroes was learning to read from Pak Trisno. He grew worried that his friend was planning to propose to Roemaisa as well. And it turned out that he was right. Djagad soon received news that the two of them had become engaged. This made Djagad so bitter with regret that he couldn't eat or sleep for days. His body had grown skinny, and his eyes had sunk into their sockets. He felt like he had no reason to go on living. Every time he saw any written words, whether it was in a magazine or on a sign in a shop window, he would feel torn apart, beaten down by the memory of losing Roemaisa. His feelings towards his dear old friend turned into hate. It was as if he himself hadn't realized how powerful his love for the girl had been.'

'But I thought our grandfather knew how to read and write!' Lebas interrupted.

'Yes, after this incident he had learned to read. Even though it was too late by then to win Roemaisa's hand,' replied Karim.

* * *

'The other thing that tormented Djagad was what had happened after Trisno's klobot business was shut down because all his capital had been confiscated by the Japanese. Pak Trisno had offered up his two remaining bales of tobacco for sale, and Djagad had headed to Magelang to look for buyers and had found someone interested in purchasing them. But when he had expressed this to Trisno, he was told that the tobacco had been sold to Idroes already.

'After this, he hated Idroes even more. And when his rival started selling his klobot in the market, Djagad's grudge against him swelled larger. He decided to leave his father's shoe business, just as his father had left his farming. He asked his father for some start-up money and then made his own klobot, to compete with Idroes. At first, he had hired a scribe to write his brand name on the packs so that the handwriting would look neat and not like chicken scratches. After a while, as his business had grown, he had made a proper package for his cigarettes, with a rectangular label and a drawing of himself on it.'

'Now, this is the label that hangs in Mas Tegar's office,' Karim said.

'It's funny, isn't it? That back then they used to put a picture of their own faces on their packs. They were so sure of themselves!' Tegar commented.

'If you make a new line of kretek, you should use a picture of your own face too!' Lebas said and burst out laughing, and Karim joined in too.

'Damn you two!' Tegar grumbled.

Karim and Lebas were laughing so hard now that Lebas had to slow the car down, his eyes wet with tears. Soon he regained control of himself, and Karim resumed narrating his story. But before he began, he issued a little warning: 'When it comes to this part of the story, I am not really sure if it happened exactly like this ...' he said. 'After all that happened, Grandfather Djagad held a massive grudge against Idroes. He even swore a lot while he was telling me this story, even though I was only just a little kid then. Our mother even reprimanded him for cursing in my presence. But I'm suspicious now as to whether the rest of the story is true, or if it all just happened in his imagination. Anyway, this is what he told me.

'Djagad heard the news that Roemaisa had been abandoned by her husband, and perhaps had become a widow. It turned out that Idroes Moeria was not a responsible husband. During the Japanese occupation, he had been running helter-skelter to hide because he was so afraid that the Japanese would capture him – and that was exactly what had happened to him. On the other hand, Djagad had played it smart, and decided to stay in town to see how things fared. In his heart, he still loved Roemaisa and was concerned about her condition. He could not bear that her husband, Djagad's sworn enemy, had left this adorable woman all alone, without taking any responsibility for her. And it turned out that as soon as Djagad came into her life, Roemaisa was happy to open her heart to him. She felt like she finally had a friend, someone she could really talk to. She was a vulnerable woman and needed a man's shoulder to lean on for strength and support. Djagad and Roemaisa had a passionate affair, to the point that he was even giving her a sum of money every month. He felt sorry for her and wanted to marry her. And she wanted to marry him too. But then, all of a sudden, Idroes returned.

'The Japanese had left, so Idroes had finally dared to come out of hiding. But in the meantime, Roemaisa had already chosen Djagad. And this was because her husband had made her wait for him, all alone, drowning in turmoil, with no certainty as to whether he was even alive. Idroes should have let Roemaisa go. Instead he challenged Djagad to a fight in the middle of the market, accusing him of violating their marriage – despite the fact that it was Idroes himself who had been a coward and hadn't taken responsibility for his wife. He proclaimed loudly to everyone in the market that if he could defeat Djagad, then Roemaisa would have to return to his embrace. If not, Djagad could have her. They came to blows and, unfortunately, Djagad had lost. Roemaisa had let herself return to her husband, even though she loved Djagad, and her heart was heavy with sorrow about leaving him.

'According to Grandfather Djagad, Roemaisa had come to him as he lay there on the ground, injured, in the middle of the market. She had tried to help him up and stop the blood pouring from his wounded nose after Idroes had beaten him up. But her husband had pulled her away cruelly, like Kurawa who had won Drupadi from Yudhistira in the Mahabharata. Djagad was heartbroken. But that was what gave him the motivation to build his clove cigarette company, so that he could defeat Idroes in business at least. And that he did.

'You can see the proof,' Karim said. 'We have never even heard of the cloves that Idroes made. Because his cigarette business never really became as successful as Grandfather Djagad's. That man was merely the king of the chicken coop ... a big fish in a small pond.'

* * *

Tegar and Lebas were listening to the story attentively.

'And we all know the rest of it.'

'Which is that our grandfather met our grandmother, and they became partners, and their business did well. Right?' Lebas confirmed.

'Yes. They met and married. Then our father, Soeraja, became the boyfriend of Purwanti, our mother, Grandfather Djagad's firstborn daughter. According to our father, he and Grandfather Djagad became business partners. And that's why our father's name was included in the brand's name, and so it became Djagad Raja cloves.'

'But how could that be? If you think about it, our grandfather and father were so far apart in age. Our father must have still been very young, yet Grandfather Djagad trusted him and accepted him as business partner?'

'Father was a prodigy, a whiz kid,' Tegar explained. 'He had a very skilled tongue that could taste the subtle differences in tobacco and sauce mixtures. So, Djagad must have been happy to accept him as partner and son-in-law.'

'Yes, that's probably what happened,' Lebas agreed, nodding. 'But didn't Mbok Marem say that our father was in a relationship with Jeng Yah?'

'Yes, she did ... But that must have been before he started seeing Mother.'

For a moment, all three brothers fell silent, each lost in their own thoughts. Then Lebas spoke. 'Wait a minute, I want to stop at this shop! I want to buy KW cigarettes as well as a pack of Djagad Raja. And who knows, maybe I'll find some more unique brands.' Lebas pulled over at a small shop and jumped out of the car excitedly. Even from inside the car, Tegar and Karim could see the rows of different kretek brands displayed in the shop's small glass window.

Tegar looked out at Lebas, who was making friendly conversation with the shop owner. Lebas had always been this way; he could be friendly with anyone.

'Do you know, Rim ...' Tegar said, but then he stopped himself.

'What, Mas?' asked Karim.

'When we were little, and Father was training me to take care of the factory and business ...'

'Yes, what about that?'

'Well, I was really jealous of you and Lebas back then. You could both play all the time and go wherever you wanted during the school holidays, while I had to work.'

Karim was stunned for a moment. He couldn't believe what he had just heard. 'But weren't you happy, Mas? You were always invited to go along with Father wherever he went. You were always travelling around with him. That's why I got all whiny and wanted to take a trip to Grandfather Djagad's house, because our father took you with him to Temanggung.'

'But at the time I was just a kid, Rim. And no kid wants to go on business trips during his school vacations. The worst part was that you two would go on holidays to Grandfather Djagad's house, while I was stuck taking care of the tobacco in Temanggung. Ugh! Lebas used to make fun of me, bragging about how he could play here and there ... So I was forced to brag that I was our father's favourite and that I was the only one who got the chance to accompany him on his trips outside the city.' Tegar's memory drifted to the first time he set foot in the Legoksari village on Sumbing Mountain, in Temanggung, where they had bought srinthil tobacco. He remembered the rows of pallets made from the dried ribs of banana stalks, piled high and lined up as containers for the tobacco to be sold. There were so many of those pallets that they had stretched up to the sky. He remembered thinking that the people of Temanggung could survive with just the two crops: tobacco and banana trees.

'But I was jealous that our father only invited you to travel with him.' Karim's words brought Tegar back to the present. Silently, he looked out the window, towards Lebas. Their kid brother could have fun anywhere. Maybe that was why, up until this very moment, the two of them had difficulty getting along.

Lebas got back in the car, grinning enthusiastically and showing them the kretek he had bought in the shop.

'Look at this, guys ... I found another clove cigarette that looks like Djagad Raja. It's called Earth in the Palm of Your Hand.' He laughed mirthfully. 'That's quite a name, isn't it?' Lebas admired the pack of cigarettes as if it was a trophy he'd just won.

Karim got behind the wheel as they headed for M Town, the city where their grandfather, Mbah Djagad, had been born. For some reason, he had the feeling that there was a missing link in the story he had just narrated, and there was something else he was yet to discover. That there was something neither their grandfather nor their father had told them. The wheels kept turning, and the car moved forward, leading them towards the denouement of the tale.

17

Cigarette Girl

M Town looked just as Lebas remembered it. Low buildings, houses painted white, wooden fences covered in peeling paint. The main road – and there was only one – stretched from one side of the town to the other, ending at the bus station, where everyone tended to congregate. A large signpost with 'M TOWN TAPE KETAN' written on it, advertising the local version of 'tape', the fermented sticky rice dish, seemed to take the place of a welcome sign. The stores selling tape ketan were unchanged – all painted in the same colour, their display cases placed in the exact same position, selling the same green-hued M Town-style tape with the same purplish mounds of sticky rice swelling up inside. The row of stores at the market were not shut up at night with metal security shutters as they were in Jakarta, but with individual wooden boards that had to be put in place one by one. Most of them had been painted, oddly, in the colour of salted eggs and then numbered, so that no matter how many times they were removed, they could be put back again in the correct order. And then there was the distinctive aroma: the smell of marl, the lime-rich red earth, still wet from a recent downpour. The city's smell of marl was always mixed with the fragrance of cloves, coming from the group of becak pedicab drivers who hung out by the side of the road in front of the market.

There were a few shops that sold wajik, sticky rice with palm sugar, the other signature snack of the town. One of them, called Mrs Pang's Wajik, sat on the left side of the street like an ancient hermit made of stone, a silent witness to all that had happened in M Town ever since the Dutch occupation. On the right side of the street was Mrs Week's Wajik, a newer store that had become popular as a purveyor of edible souvenirs. For a while, it was a competitor of Mrs Pang's Wajik. Then they were joined by Ms. Week's Wajik, which was said to have been built by Mrs Week's husband after the couple's divorce, when the family's property had been split in two.

It was as if the people who lived in this town were themselves frozen in time. M Town had been this way ever since Lebas and his brothers could remember. Since childhood, every time they visited they felt like they had returned to the same people doing the exact same things. They even got the feeling that they would still find Grandfather Djagad well and alive in his huge house. All they needed to do was turn left off the main road, Kh. A. Dalhar Street, and they would see his house there, on the left side of the street, with its large sandy front yard. There was a large square pit near the mango tree, a garbage pit; on the weekends, Lebas used to burn everything that had been thrown inside it. The terrace of the house was quite large as well, and the brothers could still almost see the shadows of the workers who used to stand there, rolling and trimming the edges of the cigarettes that were still warm in their hands.

Grandfather Djagad didn't have as many workers here in M Town as he had in Kudus. In this city, they made Proclamation cigarettes. Lebas couldn't recollect the exact year when the brand had ceased production, but he could clearly remember that it had been on the day of Eid. He and his brothers had visited Grandfather Djagad then, and the house had been surprisingly quiet and deserted. Only then had the children even realized how big the house was. They had run around as much as they had wanted, had shouted as loudly as they had wanted, until their voices had bounced off the empty walls in an echo that filled their ears.

Their car came to a stop at Grandfather Djagad's house. Kh. A. Dalhar Street was still the same, sloping downward and a little bumpy. The small shop run by an old Chinese woman was still there, and the owner was still sitting behind a glass shelf filled with matches and lighters. For some reason, she had always sold matches of the same brand, with the logo of two globes. She stocked small matches as well as large ones, the kind usually bought by food cart owners. The shop owner followed their car with her eyes until they stopped in front of Grandfather Djagad's house. Lebas noticed that she was smoking a cigarette. It seemed to him that she hadn't gotten any older, although there was a small child of about two years sitting beside her, busy teasing her. Perhaps it was her granddaughter.

The house had not changed: it was calm, with white walls. The mango tree outside was still the same – not bearing any fruit, but dropping its leaves all over the ground. It was as if the brothers could see Grandfather Djagad greeting them at the door.

The door itself was unique; it was split in half, but not down the middle and from floor-to-ceiling like most doors, so it could be opened wide, but it was split across its width, so that there was a top half and bottom half. Djagad used to greet his grandchildren by opening the top half of the door while the bottom half stayed locked. He would wave hello with a happy face, a faint cloud of smoke always hanging above his head. He was always smoking a kretek.

The brothers got out of the car. Lebas stretched himself lazily, while Tegar headed straight for the funny-looking door. But today, it remained tightly shut, and the house looked abandoned, with nothing but the cold dusty tiles to greet them. They knocked on the door.

'It seems as though there's no one here, doesn't it? It's so quiet.'

'Where's the caretaker?' Lebas asked.

'You didn't call ahead to talk to him, Bas?' Tegar said in response.

'Now, how would I know the caretaker's phone number, Mas?'

'Ah, you really can't be relied upon, can you? You are supposed to save important telephone numbers.'

'I'm not a secretary!' Lebas retorted angrily.

'Enough, enough! Shh!' Karim interjected. 'I'll call Paidi.' He was the caretaker for Grandfather Djagad's house. Out of the three brothers, only Karim had saved his telephone number, but this was not surprising because he was the most organized amongst them. And it was good thing too that he had it saved – if he didn't, they would have been stuck outside the house waiting for who knows how long.

Soon, a young man appeared, moving towards the brothers in a respectful manner. Paidi greeted them with his gentle smile and apologized that he had kept them waiting, begging their pardon and explaining that he had left the house momentarily to take his wife to the market. The brothers were only now learning that Paidi was married. To be polite, Karim asked why he hadn't sent word of the happy news to Jakarta, and the caretaker replied shyly that his wedding had been a simple affair, so far from fancy that he would have been embarrassed to invite the Soeraja family. Furthermore, in case he had even sent the invitation to their house, he wasn't sure if they would have remembered who it was inviting them. Lebas chuckled on hearing this.

'Of course we would have remembered you, Di,' Karim said, and Paidi smiled in happiness. Even Lebas had to admit that his brother truly did pay attention to each one of their employees, no matter how humble their position, and would have certainly remembered the caretaker.

While Lebas made some small talk with Paidi, the latter opened the door, having some difficulty pulling the bolt off the rusted lock of the two-piece door. They could still smell Grandfather Djagad's scent in the place as they entered the house. Perhaps his spirit still lived here, Lebas thought to himself. Paidi served them some tea in tin cups – white with military green accents and covered with matching lids to keep the tea warm and free from insects.

'Mas Paidi,' Lebas called.

'Yes, sir?'

'Do you know where we can find Lady cigarettes?'

Paidi scratched his head thoughtfully. 'Lady cigarettes, sir?'

'Yes.'

'Is that a brand of cigarette, sir?'

'Yes, of course!'

Paidi grinned. 'That's a funny name, sir.'

'But do you know where to find them?' Lebas repeated his question.

The caretaker thought about this for a moment and then shook his head. 'I don't know, sir.'

They decided to go out and ask around in the small shops around the market – perhaps the cigarettes were being sold there. They approached a number of shop owners, but none of them knew about or had even heard of Lady cigarettes. Clearly, the brand had not been sold in the market for a long time. So many different kretek companies sprung up then folded; perhaps Lady cigarettes was one of them, a brand with a short and fleeting lifespan compared to the long and enduring history of Djagad Raja cigarettes.

* * *

Dusk had fallen. It was dark, and the sounds of crickets and nocturnal creatures enlivened the air around the Djagad house. Once again, Lebas was struck by the feeling that their grandfather was still present in the house, and at any moment they would catch sight of him reading his prayers, or coming out of his bedroom with short slow steps, or sitting at the gazebo in the back and looking at the row of bonsai, which had now grown unkempt and misshapen.

'Do you have a lighter, Mas?' he asked Karim.

'I had one. It was in my jacket pocket. You can go get it ... It's in my bedroom.'

Lebas went to look for it but then returned empty handed. 'It's not there.'

'Maybe I lost it.'

'A lighter is indeed a cigarette's unreliable friend,' Lebas quipped. 'He is always disappearing, going here and there, wandering about with his elusive flame ...'

'Just go buy a new one,' Tegar snapped, annoyed. 'The little shop out front sells matches and lighters.'

'I feel lazy. Ask Paidi to do it.'

'You're too much, Lebas! How could you be too lazy for something as simple as buying a lighter?'

'What's your problem? Why are you always finding fault in me? This is wrong, that is wrong ... I'll just go to the kitchen and light my cigarette with the flame of the gas burner.' Lebas left in a huff. Tegar made it a point to show him his expression of dislike. The two brothers really were at each other's throats all the time, fighting like cat and dog.

Lebas soon returned. 'It turns out that they still use a woodstove here.'

'But don't they usually use matches for that?'

'Well, here they are ...' Lebas showed his brothers a pack of rotten, unusable matches.

'Enough of this nonsense. Just go buy a new one!' Tegar advised again.

Before Lebas could answer, Karim burst in. 'Let's go together and buy one in the shop out front. Come on.'

The two of them headed outside. Lebas took along a hooded jacket so he wouldn't get too cold. They strolled down the road, looking up at the sky.

'Wow, the stars are so clear here!' Lebas was blown away by the sight. He hadn't seen so many stars in a long time.

'In Jakarta, there are a lot of streetlamps as well as a lot of tall buildings that keep their lights on at night. All that ambient light drowns out the beams from the sky. But here it's different,' Karim explained, like he was a science teacher.

When they arrived at the shop, they saw a row of lighters and matches on display. Only after they had drawn closer, did they see the Chinese owner sitting inside the shop. Placed in the glass case near the front of the store, there were more lighters and many different brands of kretek, including Djagad Raja.

'I'd like some matches, Bu.' The Chinese lady handed Lebas a small box. 'A big one please.' She put back the small box and brought him a big one instead. He put down a twenty thousand rupiah bill, and she left to bring him back his change. 'In Jakarta nobody sells matches this big, do they?' Lebas looked at the box, opening it up and pulling out one of the giant matches. He could see the shop owner lighting a cigarette.

'Bu, what are you smoking? Djagad Raja, right?' Lebas spoke to the woman casually as if he was her good friend.

She lifted up the pack of cigarettes to show them. The brothers had never seen the brand before. It was almost empty.

'What brand is that, Bu?' Karim asked.

The shop owner stood up from her seat and walked closer, holding out the pack to them. 'It's an old-timer cigarette.'

Karim and Lebas looked at the picture of a woman on the front of the pack of cigarettes and read out the name together: 'Lady cigarettes.' They both stared at each other, their hearts pounding.

'Bu, where is this factory?'

'The factory?'

'Yes, the place where they make these cigarettes.'

'I don't know.'

'May I have these cigarettes, Bu?' The old woman just laughed in response. 'I'll buy them from you, if that's fine?'

'You can buy your own … somewhere else.' The shop owner snatched back her pack of Lady cigarettes from Lebas as if she was retrieving something incredibly valuable from his clutches.

Perhaps she thought of the two men as strange city folk and was hesitant of sharing her prized possession with them.

'Where can we buy them?' Karim enquired.

'In the market. Go all the way to the end, to the farthest corner. There's an old shop there. Right next to a store called Harmonious Rice.'

'Let's go!' Lebas said, excited.

'At this time of the night? It's sure to be closed.' The old woman cried, cutting short his enthusiasm. The brothers suddenly realized that they were in M Town, not Jakarta.

'Well, if that's the case, we'll go tomorrow morning,' Karim reassured his younger brother.

The shop owner sat back down on her chair, smiling at the brothers and exhaling her cigarette smoke. They left, heading back to Grandfather Djagad's house, where they excitedly informed Tegar that Lady cigarettes were still being sold in the market, but that only the old folks in M Town smoked them.

The next morning, at seven, the three brothers woke up. Or, more precisely, Tegar and Karim woke up. Lebas was still lazing in bed. Paidi was preparing porridge for them, with gudeg krecek, or stewed jackfruit, as side dish; this was the kind of porridge they used to eat for breakfast as children. But when Lebas overheard Tegar asking Karim to wake him up, he got up of his own accord and hurried to the bathroom for a shower.

They headed straight to the small shop at the edge of the market, just as the Chinese shop owner had directed them. They looked for the Harmonious Rice store, but the place looked more like a house than a shop, with piles of old things strewn around and emanating a strange odour from within. Out of the corner of their eyes, the brothers spotted piles of betel chew and leaves, and deduced that it was perhaps a sirih store. They spotted an old Chinese man sitting there – but the word 'old' didn't do him justice. 'Ancient' was a more fitting description. He was a relic, like a piece of Chinese porcelain that had been buried in the ocean for centuries.

'It's like I can read the city's history in his eyes,' Lebas whispered, giggling. 'If only I could see his eyes though ... I can't be sure if they are open or closed. And if they are open, I wonder whether he can still see, or whether his sight has been ravaged by cataracts.' Tegar glared at his brother and gestured for him to stop speaking.

The old man was sitting there motionless, as if guarding his shop. His head was bald, and there were a few dark patches on his scalp. One single strand of hair was growing out of his head, waiting to fall out, as if it was left there just to demonstrate how old he is. He was wearing nothing but a loose undershirt. There was a cane resting against the wall not far from where he was sitting. A fly buzzed towards his oily eyes, landing on one of the closed puffy lids. He didn't bother swatting it away.

'We'd like to buy something!' Lebas called out to him. The Chinese man didn't move. The brothers looked at each other uncomfortably, afraid he had died right there in his chair.

'Excuse me, sir. We'd very much like to buy something!' This time, Tegar spoke in Javanese and in a purposefully loud voice, in case the man hadn't heard them before.

Suddenly, a younger Chinese man walked into the shop. Perhaps he was the old man's son – or his grandchild, or perhaps his great grandchild.

'What would you like?' he asked politely in Javanese. 'Would you like some sirih?'

'No, thank you,' Tegar replied. 'We are not looking for sirih. We are looking for Lady cigarettes.'

'Lady cigarettes?'

'Yes,' Tegar nodded confidently, 'you sell Lady cigarettes, don't you?'

The younger Chinese man approached the ancient one. 'Grandpa Uyut, do we sell Lady cigarettes?' He addressed the older man as Grandpa Uyut, which meant the latter was indeed his great-grandfather.

Then, a surprising thing happened: the ancient man moved. He got up from his woven rattan chair, which was riddled with holes. As he stood, the chair let out a creak so loud it became apparent that the piece of furniture was just as old as the person using it. Tegar, Karim and Lebas were left startled by the man's sudden movement. The fly that had been resting comfortably on the old man's face buzzed away – perhaps it was just as surprised as they were. The man turned slowly, heading towards a messy corner of the shop. The younger man helped him as he sifted through the goods piled up there. Then, he found the Lady cigarettes, and took out a pack and gave it to Tegar.

'Can we buy a whole carton?' Lebas asked, but Tegar immediately interrupted him.

'What do you need a whole carton for?'

'For no special reason ... Just as a souvenir.'

'A souvenir? You think we are on a vacation here?' Tegar was getting annoyed. 'Just one pack,' he said to the young man. 'How much do I owe you?'

'How much does it cost, Grandfather?' The old man took a small piece of chalk and wrote a number on the wooden table with a trembling hand. 'Four thousand five hundred,' the younger man read out loud.

Lebas noticed that the price tag on the Lady cigarettes box said 3,500 rupiah for a pack of twelve. He realized that these men were earning a fairly significant profit, yet weren't getting rich. He took the pack from Tegar's hand and read from it: 'Produced by Idroes Moeria, M Town-Indonesia.'

'So these cigarettes are made locally? Do you know where the factory is?' Tegar enquired.

The young Chinese man shrugged. 'Perhaps my grandfather knows.' He approached the old man again and moved his mouth close to his ear to repeat the question. To the brothers, the old man's answer sounded muffled, like a bunch of confused bees. 'He says that Lady cigarettes aren't made here in M Town anymore,' the young man reported and then he moved his ear to his grandfather's mouth. 'He says they are made in Magelang now.'

'Magelang?'

'Really, in Magelang?'

'That's what my great-grandfather says.'

And so the brothers headed next for Magelang.

* * *

They hadn't even been driving for an hour when they reached the small town of Magelang.

'But where can we find the Lady cigarette factory?'

'Ask a local. Maybe they'll know.' Lebas pointed towards a small shop by the side of the road, and Karim pulled up there. Lebas got out and bought a bottle of water, using this as an excuse to strike up conversation with the shopkeeper. He saw a row of cloves displayed on a small rack stocked exclusively with cigarettes, and noticed that Lady cigarettes were being sold here as well – apparently, in this city these cigarettes were easy to find, probably because they were made here – and that they had been placed right next to the Djagad Raja's packs.

'And one pack of Lady cigarettes, please,' Lebas said, picking one off the rack.

'You're not from around here, are you, little brother?'

'That's right. I'm from Jakarta.'

'Wow, that's far!'

'How could you tell, Bu?'

'People from around here speak Javanese, and they almost never buy Lady cigarettes.' The woman chuckled.

'Oh really?'

'Yes, the only ones who buy those cigarettes are the old folks who have been smoking them for a long time.'

'Oh, I see. Do you happen to know where the Lady cigarette factory is?'

'Yes, I do.' Lebas grinned from ear to ear on hearing this. 'Keep going in this direction ... you'll come to a junction by the rice fields. Take a right there, son. Then keep going straight until you see a house with a mosque next door to it. That's the place you're looking for.'

Lebas's grin vanished in astonishment. 'Seriously, Bu? That's the Lady cigarette factory?'

'Yes.'

He immediately rushed back to the car and informed his brothers. All of them were amazed; it was such a lucky coincidence that the shopkeeper knew where the factory was located, and it wasn't even too far away. They followed the route the shop owner gave them, and sure enough they found the lovely house with a large yard and a mosque next door. A small nameplate in front of the house read 'PR. IDROES MOERIA' and had the Lady cigarette logo displayed on it. The PR. stood for Perusahaan Rokok, or Cigarette Company.

As the brothers stepped out of the car, a sweet young girl peered out from the mosque, and then she came down the steps carrying a mukena, her prayer robe, which she hadn't had the chance to fold yet.

'Assalamu'alaikum,' Karim greeted her.

'Wa'ailaikum salam. Who are you?' she replied.

'My name is Karim. This is my older brother, Tegar, and my younger brother, Lebas.'

'May I help you with something?' she asked politely.

'We have come here looking for Jeng Yah.'

'Oh, Jeng Yah. Just a moment. Please come in.'

The three of them followed her mutely into the front room of the house. They were feeling a bit overwhelmed. They couldn't believe that they were finally about to meet Jeng Yah, the woman their father had been calling out for on his deathbed. An old sepia photograph hung on the wall, showing the face of an elderly man. Perhaps this was Idroes Moeria. There was another photograph on the table, also sepia-toned, of two young women.

The girl disappeared inside, and then reappeared with a middle-aged woman: Jeng Yah.

'Yes? I heard you were looking for me?'

The brothers looked at each other. She was just an ordinary looking woman with a motherly face. In fact, she looked to be about the same age as their own mother.

'You are Jeng Yah?'

'Yes, I'm Jeng Yah.'

'We are looking for you because our father would like to meet you.'

'Your father? And who is that?'

'Pak Raja.'

Jeng Yah pondered over this for a moment. 'Raja? As in, Soeraja?' she said finally.

'Yes!' The three of them answered eagerly in unison.

'The same Soeraja who owns Djagad Raja clove cigarettes?'

'Yes!' they cried together again, thrilled.

Jeng Yah smiled at them and then sat down. 'The person you are looking for is my older sister, not me. Her name was Dasiyah, and mine is Rukayah. We're both called Jeng Yah.' The brothers' excitement drained away as they heard this. 'Where is Mas Raja now?'

'In Jakarta. He's very sick, and he keeps saying that he wants to see Jeng Yah. Can you tell us where the other Jeng Yah is now? Your older sister?' Tegar asked.

'Please have a seat first. What's your name?'

'Tegar. I am Pak Raja's eldest son.'

'Arum!' Jeng Yah called out.

'Yes, mother?' The young girl responded.

'Make three cups of tea please, will you?' Arum, the young girl from the mosque, left to prepare tea for the guests. And then Jeng Yah began to tell the brothers a story. 'I still remember the first time I met Mas Raja ...'

* * *

'Soeraja was a free spirit. He captured my older sister's heart with his stories of travel and adventure. Yah's eyes would shine brightly whenever she spoke of Mas Raja. Everything was going smoothly, and our father Idroes Moeria had even given them his blessing. But then Mas Raja got mixed up with the PKI, the Communist party.

'It was believed that when the PKI was actively recruiting a lot of people, and their propaganda was everywhere, Mas Raja received some money to make a brand of cigarettes for them, a brand that the party would produce and sell. He called them Red Sickle cigarettes. After the generals were murdered in what was thought to be an attempted Communist coup, followed by the obliteration of the Communist party everywhere, Mas Raja was implicated too. Everyone knew who made Red Sickle kretek because it was written right there on the box: "Made by the Soeraja Factory in M Town".

'Soeraja became an easy target; no matter how emphatically he declared he was not involved in the political activities of the Communist party, his name was still on the list of people to be punished. Mas Raja was forced to leave M Town in order to save his own life. My older sister became a target too, as did my father, and they were taken in for questioning. Independence! cigarettes, which was better established than Lady cigarettes at the time, was accused of being associated with the PKI too. They made these allegations because Independence! used red paper – red like blood, red like the colour that dominated all the PKI propaganda. And this was despite the fact that my father had created his brand during the time of independence and had no relationship to any political party whatsoever.

'Father was finally freed after he promised to shut down Independence! and Yah was freed because of her popularity as the "cigarette girl" from Lady cigarettes. She was renowned for possessing the unique gift of sweet spit – people said the cloves she rolled by hand tasted exceptionally delicious because she used her spit to seal them. My father and my older sister were both very lucky that they were acquitted and allowed to return home.

'For a while, our family didn't make any cigarettes at all. We didn't even produce Lady cigarettes, although we still had permission to do so. We decided to be cautious – all we wanted was to stay safe and avoid any trouble. We took it day by day, living off our father's savings.

'As for my sister, Dasiyah … She grew skinny, and she lost her appetite, and she didn't even want to drink anything. She was beside herself thinking about Mas Raja. She wanted to find out where he was, but she didn't dare speak his name out loud or ask anyone about him, because if she went looking for him, then she would have been suspected again of being involved with the PKI party. Almost a year after the purported coup and its gruesome aftermath, a letter arrived from Kudus. It turned out that Mas Raja was there. That letter gave my sister hope again. At the very least, she knew now that her future husband was safe.

'Dasiyah and Mas Raja sent each other more letters, and she eventually learned that the person hiding him was Pak Djagad, your grandfather. Djagad had started Proclamation cigarettes in M Town initially, but had decided to move to Kudus to develop his business. It seemed like Mas Raja had intentionally asked Pak Djagad for help. I wasn't surprised – they must have already known each other when they both lived in M Town. But, you must know that Mas Raja had been our father's trusted right-hand man, and it was certain that our father or Dasiyah *must* have told him about the business rivalry between them and Pak Djagad. Yet, in spite of being aware of this history, Mas Raja wrote to my sister about how Pak Djagad had invited him to form a partnership and create a new brand of kretek together. When she heard of this, Dasiyah was happy for her sweetheart. But Soeraja still didn't dare leave Kudus, because he feared that if he got too far away from Pak Djagad, and no longer had anyone to protect him, he would be captured. The government was still actively looking for anyone who had been involved with the Communist party. Even the wives and children of those suspected were being hunted. But Dasiyah tried to stay hopeful, and chose to focus on Mas Raja's safety.

'Soon after that, Djagad Raja cigarettes were introduced in M Town and sold in our market. You could find them everywhere. I bought a pack for Dasiyah. She smiled when she saw them, but then burst into tears. I asked her what was wrong, and at first she said she was crying tears of joy, because Mas Raja had finally started his own kretek company and created his own product, just as he had always dreamed ... But I knew there was something else. Then Dasiyah showed me his letter, and in it Mas Raja had asked for her forgiveness because he was forced to end their relationship. In order to ensure both their safety, he had to stay back in Kudus, and he didn't know for how long. He also confessed to her that he had not been faithful to her or their love. All this time that he had been away, there had been another woman in his life, to whom he had been confiding all his troubles, and who in turn had been listening patiently to him. He was going to marry Purwanti, Pak Djagad's eldest daughter. The letter ended with him begging for her forgiveness and saying that he still truly loved her and that he wished the situation had been different and that they could have been together. Soeraja informed my sister that his wedding to Purwanti was to happen only two days later ...

'Dasiyah cried her heart out after she had finished reading the letter. But she said she didn't want to do anything about the wedding. All she wanted was for Mas Raja to be safe and happy. She tried to smile through her tears. To console her, I opened the pack of Djagad Raja clove cigarettes I had bought and offered her a kretek. I knew that she would calm down a little after having a smoke. She accepted the cigarette, and I lit it for her, and then lit my own cigarette. I told her that it was all right if she felt angry about everything that had happened. But my sister wasn't listening ... She had barely begun smoking when she wiped the tears from her eyes, stood up and threw away the cigarette, still burning, onto the floor. It was as if, just by smoking that kretek, she had gathered her courage. She said that she was going to give Mas Raja a piece of her mind. And that very afternoon, she packed a bag and walked to the M Town bus terminal. She went straight to Kudus. Father, Mother and I had forbade her from going, but she insisted. She didn't stay in Kudus for very long, two nights at most, then returned home. I recall her telling us, still fuming, "I hit Soeraja on his forehead with a kerosene lamp ... on his wedding day!" I remember she laughed hysterically, but she was weeping at the same time. She had felt victorious, but also pathetic. He must have looked really awful on his wedding day, with the stitches and bandages around his head.

'The very next day, Dasiyah threw herself back into making Lady cigarettes. She recalled all the rollers and trimmers and they resumed their work.'

* * *

The three brothers sat speechless after hearing the story.

'So, where is Jeng Yah now?' Karim finally asked.

'Jeng Yah, Dasiyah, my beloved older sister who you are seeking …' Rukayah said sadly, 'died in childbirth.'

'Died? *Died*!' Lebas murmured in disbelief. He leaned in to whisper to Karim, 'So we have come all the way here just to discover that the Jeng Yah we are searching for is long gone.' Karim ignored his brother and focussed instead on the Jeng Yah sitting before them.

'So who did Jeng Yah the First marry?' Lebas asked. The Jeng Yah before them smiled on hearing this. This would make her 'Jeng Yah the Second'.

'She married a good man called Sugeng. But she was already over thirty by then – she was thirty-two, to be exact. I was married nine years before she was. Their marriage only lasted one year. Jeng Yah died in labour,' Rukayah said.

Suddenly Arum, who had been quiet all this time, spoke. 'I am Dasiyah's child …'

'Yes, this is Arum Cengkeh, my sister's daughter,' said Jeng Yah.

Arum Cengkeh. Fragrant Clove, that was what the girl's name meant.

'You have a great name,' Lebas said, and Arum smiled at the compliment. Tegar rolled his eyes towards the ceiling. Even at a time like this, his brother had managed to find a chance to flirt with somebody's daughter.

'Yes, I'm really Arum's aunt. But I have cared for her as if she were my own child, especially because all of my own children are boys,' Rukayah continued. Arum smiled at the brothers, and they could see then, in that instance, that Jeng Yah the First would have looked as sweet as her daughter.

They said their goodbyes, but before they could leave, Lebas took the opportunity to talk to Arum for a little while and exchange phone numbers with her.

'Classic Lebas!' Tegar grumbled crankily under his breath, but his brother didn't care and continued talking to Arum.

Karim's mobile lit up suddenly. 'Mother's calling,' he said and answered the call. 'Yes, Mother?'

They could hear their mother's voice through the phone, and she sounded panicked and was practically screaming, 'Karim, you have to come home right away! Your father has had a heart attack!' Then she hung up.

The brothers exchanged worried glances. They rushed to their car. They drove immediately, heading back towards Yogyakarta as quickly as they could, so they could catch the next flight home to Jakarta.

18
Fragrant Cloves

Soeraja was dying. And at the end of his life, he was still calling out a name: Jeng Yah. But now, unlike four days ago, his children knew that Jeng Yah was dead.

Perhaps she had come to him, a face from his past, a ghost born from his guilt, a reminder of the love he had so carelessly abandoned. His wife was weeping, consumed by jealousy and grief, knowing that her husband was gravely ill and would soon pass away.

'Mother,' Karim said to her. Lebas approached them, eavesdropping on their conversation. Their mother was trying to get control of herself.

'So, did you find her?'

Karim shook his head. 'Jeng Yah is dead.'

Their mother was startled. She searched Karim's face, looking for reassurance. 'She's dead?'

'Yes,' he said with certainty. 'We went all the way to Magelang to look for her. But we found that she has been dead for a long time now.'

Their mother wept again, but this time, her sons didn't know what her tears meant. Perhaps she was disappointed that Jeng Yah was dead, or perhaps she was relieved, or perhaps she was angry because this meant that Soeraja would be reunited with

Jeng Yah soon when he crossed over to the other side.

'Jeng Yah was our father's old girlfriend, wasn't she?' asked Karim. Their mother nodded. 'And Jeng Yah hit him with a kerosene lamp on your wedding day, didn't she?'

Their mother nodded again. She was weeping louder. 'That woman was jealous,' she said through her sobs, 'because your father chose me over her.' She addressed Jeng Yah as 'her' and 'that woman', refusing to speak her name.

The nurse suddenly called for them. They all rushed into Soeraja's room. Tegar had his hand on his father's forehead, whispering the names of Allah the All Powerful. Soon, a choking sound escaped Soeraja's throat. He let out his last breath, and then he was gone.

* * *

His death was big news: Soeraja, the owner of the Djagad Raja cigarette dynasty, had returned home to meet his maker. The process of bathing him, praying over his body and burying him was carried out quickly. The media hounded Tegar for his comments, and he answered as the family spokesperson and future leader of Djagad Raja cigarettes. Everyone knew that if Djagad Raja was a kingdom, then Tegar was its crown prince, and the throne would be passed down to him.

Lebas retreated from the onslaught of the press. They wanted to interview him too, the youngest mourning son who was fairly well known in their circles for making B and C class films with the names of ghouls and demons in their titles. However, even though he was quite comfortable handling a camera, Lebas didn't like to be in front of it.

He slipped away and found refuge in an empty room, free from the press and the frenetic barrage of condolences. He hadn't taken a bath in two days, or even had the chance to change his clothes. Meeting Jeng Yah the Second and uncovering his father's past, and then finally seeing his father pass away had all been too overwhelming for him. Lebas felt around in his pocket and found a familiar object: a pack of clove cigarettes. He took it out, hoping for it to be a Djagad Raja, which he usually smoked, but then discovered he was wrong. It was a pack of Lady cigarettes. He recollected that he had bought them the day before in M Town. He smiled, remembering the words of the shop owner, about how this brand was smoked by the elderly and not meant for young guys like him. He opened the pack, taking out one cigarette and lighting it with one of the big matches he had bought in M Town. He inhaled deeply and ... Lebas was dumbfounded. He quickly took another drag, just to be sure. It was true! There was no way he was mistaken.

He emerged quickly from his hideaway and found Tegar. His brother was still surrounded by journalists. Lebas pushed through the mob to reach him.

'Mas! I have to talk to you!'

'In a minute,' whispered Tegar.

'Now, Mas!'

'In a minute!' he snapped, still whispering.

Lebas had to wait. Impatiently, he lit himself another Lady cigarette. When Tegar was finally done with the media, he came to find him, grumbling. 'What's going on with you? Didn't you see that I was busy? Look at the situation and act accordingly, man!'

'Yeah, Mas, okay, okay ... Here, try this,' Lebas popped the

Lady cigarette he'd just lit into Tegar's mouth.

'What is this?' his brother sputtered.

'Try it, Mas. Just try it,' Lebas insisted.

Tegar wrinkled his forehead in annoyance, certain that his brother was being ridiculous. But he did what Lebas asked of him anyway. He smoked the cigarette.

'What? It's just a regular Djagad cigarette. There's nothing strange about it–'

'That's not a Djagad Raja, Mas!' Lebas interrupted. His brother fell silent and then looked down at the rolling paper in his hand.

'Lady cigarettes?' he asked, surprised. Lebas nodded. His brother took another drag, 'This is really a Lady cigarette?'

'Yes, Mas!'

Karim approached them. 'What's going on?'

'Try it, Rim!' Tegar held out the cigarette. Karim inhaled it.

'It's our cigarette. Tastes normal to me. What is so special about it?'

'But you're wrong!' Lebas said, all riled up. 'That's a Lady cigarette!' Karim gaped down at the cigarette in his hand and noticed the logo.

'But ... it tastes just like ours! It must be an imitation of our Djagad Raja brand.'

'Mas, do you remember what Jeng Yah the Second told us the other day? Lady cigarettes was first started in M Town, and then Djagad Raja cigarettes came after that, right?' As Tegar and Karim listened to him, the scattered pieces of the puzzle finally began to come together in their heads. 'Our father earned Idroes Moeria's trust. He worked with him, making Lady cigarettes, and he even had a romantic relationship with Jeng Yah the First.

Perhaps he was made privy to the formula of the sauce for Lady cigarettes, which were the most popular at the time and became the number one brand in M Town, Central Java and Yogyakarta. And perhaps, later, when he formed a partnership with Grandfather Djagad, our father divulged to him the recipe for the secret Lady cigarette sauce. That's why he was made partner and his name was printed on the pack, even though he didn't have any financial stake in the company,' Lebas explained breathlessly.

Tegar and Karim were silent, mulling over their brother's analysis. But there was more. 'And maybe ...' Lebas paused.

'What?' Tegar asked impatiently.

'Maybe, Jeng Yah didn't whack our father's head with the kerosene lamp because she was jealous. Don't you remember? Jeng Yah the Second said that her sister wanted to go to Kudus straightaway after smoking a Djagad Raja cigarette ... Perhaps, Jeng Yah the First didn't come to the wedding because she wanted to exact revenge on our father for marrying another woman. I think she was shocked when she smoked the Djagad Raja cigarette. Because it tasted exactly like her own brand. And she knew there could only be one explanation: our father had stolen the secret formula and given it to Grandfather Djagad!'

'Oh my God! This means that all this time, our business ...' Karim turned pale and collapsed into a chair, trying to control his feelings. 'This means we have partaken of something haram, something sinful, my brothers. We have lived off stolen money.'

'And we have never taken any responsibility, Mas ... Meanwhile, this theft has made us rich enough for seven generations,' Lebas said. 'It's like we have stolen a magic charm and used it to grow wealthy,' he added to lighten the mood.

None of the brothers knew what to do. They thought of their

father, who had just been laid in the ground. His secret would have followed him to the grave had Lebas not smoked the Lady cigarette.

Perhaps, Soeraja had wanted to see Jeng Yah because he had been hounded by his sin: the sin of stealing a secret recipe, and betraying the trust of a loved one.

* * *

Forty days after their father's death, Tegar summoned Lebas to his office. The younger brother was seated before Tegar's desk, looking solemn and feeling uncomfortable, as if he was at a job interview.

'Do you still want to make that film?' Tegar asked.

Lebas was confused for a moment, unable to believe his brother's words. 'Yes!' he managed to say finally. Enthusiastically, he took out his laptop, eager to show Tegar his presentation.

'You don't have to do that. Just send me your presentation later. I don't want to see it now.' Lebas was disappointed. He hadn't even had the chance to turn on his laptop. 'I want to talk to you about something else. About Djagad Raja ...'

'What about that?' Lebas said sullenly, putting away his computer.

'I want you to make me a commercial for Djagad Raja.' Lebas could not believe his ears. He was stunned. 'Tell me your concept. If it sounds OK, then we'll proceed with it,' Tegar continued.

'Are you serious?'

'Do I look like I'm joking?' Lebas shook his head quickly. 'You said you wanted a chance to become a serious filmmaker, didn't you? That you just didn't want to keep making films about evil spirits and ghosts?'

'Right.'

'So, prove to me that you can make a good commercial. I want something that captures the energy of Djagad Raja's growth. Something that is very Indonesian.'

'I'm ready, Mas. I'm going to go think about the concept right away.'

'But first …' Tegar took out an envelope. 'I've got another job for you.'

'What is it?'

'Deliver this.' Tegar pushed the envelope towards his brother. Lebas opened it to find a piece of paper with a familiar name on it. 'Deliver this tomorrow, while you are thinking about the concept for the commercial. Do you understand?'

'Yes, Mas.' He got up and made for the reception area.

'Lebas!' Tegar called. His brother stopped and turned around. 'There better not be any mummies or she-devils in the ad, got it?'

'Got it!' Lebas grinned. Tegar's laughter followed him out of the office.

* * *

The next day, Lebas woke up early to carry out Tegar's order. He flew to Yogyakarta on the early morning flight. Then he rented himself a car and drove to Magelang. His brother had sent him to meet Jeng Yah the Second.

Sweet Arum greeted him at the door. She was expecting him; they had been sending each other text messages since they had last met, and Lebas had even called to inform her that his father had passed away. The previous night he had contacted her again to tell her he would be paying them a visit and to check if she and Jeng Yah the Second would be home.

'Come in, Mas. Oh ...' Arum searched behind him for the others. 'You've come alone? Where are Mas Tegar and Mas Karim?'

'They haven't come along.'

Arum invited him in to have a seat, then left for a moment. She reappeared with a small tray of tea and little glasses. 'The last time you were here I didn't have the chance to serve you anything, did I? Now, please, have some tea.' She realized Lebas would be thirsty after his long journey.

'Is your mother home?' he asked.

'Just a moment. I'll call her for you.' Arum went in again.

Lebas waited, drinking the tea that had been served to him. He picked up the little cup: the picture on it interested him. He paused to look at it more closely. Three Ball cigarettes. The brand had stopped production way back in the 1950s, but this family still owned a souvenir tea set. What was even more amazing, it wasn't being preserved carefully like the antique it was, but rather it was still being used. This was probably a family heirloom, he decided. He admired the pot and the cute little cups. The only time he had ever seen anything like this was years ago at the Cigarette Museum in Kudus.

Soon, Jeng Yah the Second walked into the room, and he hurriedly put down the little cup. He noticed that her eyes still held the same peaceful expression they had when he had first met her more than a month ago.

'My condolences. I saw the news of Mas Raja's death on the television,' she said. Lebas nodded and thanked her. Then, in explanation for his sudden visit, he presented the envelope to her.

'This is from Mas Tegar. I'm sorry only I was able to come here today. Mas Tegar and Mas Karim will visit another time, when their work permits.'

Jeng Yah opened the envelope and read the formal letter of apology from Djagad Raja cigarettes, asking for forgiveness for stealing the sauce recipe from Lady cigarettes and explaining how the three brothers, Soeraja's descendants, regretted that they had only just realized what had happened. The letter ended by stating their intentions to formally buy the Lady cigarette formula as well as the assets of the Lady cigarette company, in order to develop it as a brand managed by the Djagad Raja Corporation. Jeng Yah was taken aback.

'You want to buy our company?'

'Yes, we do,' Lebas said. 'Please consider our offer.'

Then he took out another envelope and handed it to her. Jeng Yah opened it, and this time found a cheque for 1,000,000,000 rupiah addressed to her. 'That is what we are offering to pay you for the Lady cigarette sauce formula,' Lebas explained.

Jeng Yah the Second sat there bewildered, not knowing what to say. She looked at Arum and asked, 'So, how about it, Rum? What do you think we should do? This cigarette company belonged to your late mother, you know.' Arum looked back and forth between Jeng Yah the Second and Lebas, considering the offer.

'It's alright, Mother. It is time we let go, don't you think? We've had enough of taking care of Lady cigarettes,' she said. Jeng Yah the Second looked at Lebas and nodded, agreeing with Arum.

Lebas savoured this moment. He was happy that he was finally able to clean up the mess his family had caused. He would never have imagined that he, the black sheep of the family, would be the one to end up doing something so worthwhile. He took a Lady cigarette from his pocket and offered it to Jeng Yah. She smiled.

'I haven't had one in a very long while ... But now seems like the right time for it.' Jeng Yah took the cigarette and placed it between her lips. Lebas clicked the lighter. The flame licked the tip of the cigarette, and the kretek-kretek of burning cloves could be heard crackling in the peaceful quiet of their hearts.